MW00905845

# FOR THE LOVE OF STRANGERS

## By Jacqueline Horsfall

### Illustrated by Mary B. Kelly

Happy reading!...
Cassidy...
Jacqueline
Horsfall
Fall
2010

For the Love of Strangers

Contact Information: info@leapbks.com

Interior Art by *Mary B. Kelly*
Cover Art "Russian Deer Goddess: Rozhanitza"
© Mary B. Kelly
Used by kind permission of the artist

Leap Books
Powell, WY
www.leapbks.com

Publishing History
First Leap Edition 2010
ISBN: 978-1-61603-003-2

LCCN  2010937608

Published in the United States of America

**FOR THE LOVE OF STRANGERS** instantly drew me into this poignant tale of a Russian adoptee, then continued to intrigue as it masterfully interwove threads of past and present into a haunting, lyrical novel that echoes in the heart and mind long after the pages are closed.

~Patricia Hermes, award-winning author of *You Shouldn't Have to Say Goodbye, Mama, Let's Dance*, and *Dear America/ My America* series

# Dedication

For Nicholas, my Nikolai

# THEN

*Ants in my pants.*

That's what Tee-tee found when she stripped off my tattered jumper to bathe me. Well, not literally ants. *Worms*, to be exact. Thriving in my soiled panties, along with a colony of other parasites, all courtesy of the Moscow Home for Abandoned Children. We joke about it now, but at the time I was clueless as to why this scowling stranger had whisked me away from my prison, dropped shiny tin-foiled chocolate kisses into my lap as we sped past the Kremlin wall, then stripped me naked in the privacy of her hotel bathroom and pushed me away,

repulsed. Accepted and spurned in one short afternoon, and etched into my memory to this day, preserved like lifeless petals from a plucked daisy: *She loves me, she loves me not.*

That was ten years ago, the day Tee-tee got saddled with me. I was a scrawny six-year-old huddled on the grimy cement steps of a drab two-story warehouse, the door flanked by enormous posters of Grandfather Lenin raising a fist in victory. A ragtag team of boys playing kickball scattered as a *taksi* pulled into the yard, the letter *T* stamped in a checkered design on the door, its green light off signifying a passenger inside. The door opened, and a stout, gray-haired woman wearing blinding-white sneakers stepped out, clutching papers and photos. A shiny black purse trimmed with gold braid was slung over her shoulder.

Whispers carried across the play yard. *Babushka.* Grandmother.

A thrill of anticipation swept over us. The only visitors to our orphanage had been aloof, impassive government bureaucrats with clipboards in their hands. But this gray-haired woman was not a black-suited, clipboard-toting official. To us, she was a *babushka*, a grandmother. But whose? Which of us would be

leaving with her, going home?

We silently gawked at her while she surveyed the dirt playground, sniffed and grimaced, and turned back to the *taksi*. This obviously was a wrong stop, our pathetic mudhole filled with unkempt kids. Surely any grandmother who could afford snow-white sneakers, a trendy handbag, and a *taksi* ride from the city would not be searching for her own blood here. I turned my face to a shaft of sunlight and closed my eyes, not letting myself hope for something that could never be. She would leave alone. I was sure of it.

The orphanage director, Mr. Petrov, bustled through the door, nearly tumbling over me. He strode across the yard, booming greetings at the gray-haired woman. He clasped her hand, doing his best to communicate with dramatic arm thrusts, punctuated by sounds I didn't understand.

English, it turned out to be. American English.

The woman turned back to the *taksi* driver, pointed to her wristwatch, then flashed ten fingers twice, signaling instructions: *Twenty minutes*. The driver shrugged and flicked his cigarette out the window.

Director Petrov barked orders at the staff,

and we were hustled inside. The aides dusted off our clothes, tidied braids and bangs, spit-shined cheeks. We stood shoulder to shoulder, lined up against the cool corridor walls.

The gray-haired woman smiled and nodded at us, then handed the director her papers and photos. No, not photos of me. Nor any of the other kids my age lined up with me along the walls. I didn't know it at the time, but I soon discovered the photos were of my seven-month-old brother, Nikolai.

Director Petrov whispered to his assistant, then clapped his hands. A moment later Nikky was carried from the nursery and handed over. Howling, he twisted and clung to Anya, the nursery aide. She cooed and shushed with bouncy motions, prying his pudgy fingers from her neck. Nikky stiffened and shrieked in a baby meltdown.

A cheer rallied inside me. *Scream, Nikky. Stay here with me. Don't go.*

The gray-haired woman rummaged madly through her large black purse. She exhaled in relief as she withdrew her offering—a plush yellow duck wearing a Yankees cap.

She squeezed it. *Quack.*

Nikky's wailing stopped mid-shriek. His watery blue eyes crinkled. Two teeth gleamed in

a big grin. Bribe accepted. He went willingly into the woman's embrace, pressing his silky cheek against her creased one.

"*Nyet,*" I cried out. Nikky was the only family I had left. He was my life. I would die without him.

Director Petrov looked up sharply. He scanned the corridor until he focused on me. Our eyes locked.

"Darya." My name echoed down the hall. "*Iditye syouda,*" he ordered with the wave of his hand.

I crept toward him, keeping my eyes glued on my grimy toes.

"Darya?" he said again, softly this time.

I looked up. Nikky was cooing at his fluffy new friend, mushing his face in the yellow fur. He didn't even notice me. My heart plummeted to the scarred linoleum.

Director Petrov took my hand. "Sister," he said, turning to the woman. "You take?"

Her mouth dropped open in a large *O.* She cased me up and down, shifting her gaze from me to the director and back. I read the reluctance on her face, in her furrowed brow and scowl. She didn't really want me. She'd come for a baby and gotten a baby. Why did she need a tag-along girl?

Finally, she pursed her lips and blew out a breath. She shifted Nikky to her other hip. "Darya?" She touched my shoulder, then pointed to her chest. "Tee-tee." She squeezed out a thin smile.

I followed her to Director Petrov's office. She signed papers to remove Nikolai and Darya Malakovsky from Russia. Two for the price of one.

As our *taksi* sped toward the Hotel Moskva, my eyes teared up, but I clamped my mouth shut, refusing to wail. I did and did not want to leave. I was gaining Nikky but losing the only home I knew. Would I ever again see the cobblestones of Red Square, the shops on Gorky Street, the onion-domes of St. Basil's Cathedral?

What choice did I have?

The hotel room with its two small twin beds was twice the size of my orphanage room that slept eight. I inspected each corner of the room and the small closet, and peered under the beds. Where were the others who shared this room? Surely all this space wasn't for just the three of us. But when I turned to Tee-tee and pointed at the beds, then counted eight on my fingers, she merely shrugged and dumped the contents of her large purse over one of the bedspreads. How would we communicate if even sign language was useless?

I inched toward the wide window. Traffic surged below. The streetlights flickered on as the sun dipped low. A wave of nausea swept over me. I had never been so high. While Nikky napped on a bed shoved against the wall, Tee-tee ran bath water and coaxed me into the bathroom. I jerked away when she tried to remove my jumper and huddled against the cool white tile behind the toilet.

"Ummm," she crooned, dipping her hand in the water, patting it on her face. "Warm. Nice." She unwrapped a small bar of soap and held it under her nose. "Ummm," she soothed, inhaling. "Nice." She dropped the soap in the tub. It floated!

Oh, how I wanted to play with the floating soap smelling of honeysuckle and immerse myself in the warm water. A memory, soft as a moth's wing, brushed my thoughts. Of the pond at our summer *dacha*, me clinging to my father's neck as he sculled water, a dragonfly flitting about his head. I felt safe with him, unlike this woman who might very likely drown me.

The soap won. I scuttled across the tiled floor and let her undress me. She examined my skin, front and back, running her fingers over the red bumps. Then she picked my panties off the bathroom floor, stretched the waistband, and looked inside. Her mouth twisted in disgust. She flung them toward the trash basket. In an instant I was plunged into the water, Tee-tee's hand soaping between my legs. I was too scared to scream.

Grunting, Tee-tee pushed off her knees and hobbled to her suitcase. She returned with a soft cotton shirt over her arm. I lolled in the tub while Tee-tee scrubbed my hair, digging her fingers into my scalp. She toweled me dry, slid the baggy shirt over my head, and rolled up the sleeves. She swung me up onto the bed with Nikky, unfolded a paper diaper, lifted my hips, and taped it around my skinny bottom. Humiliated, I shrieked and ripped it off, then

flung it across the room. Tee-tee made a grab for me, but I dove under bed and wriggled further under the bed frame, away from her grasp. But Tee-tee's fingers caught my ankle and dragged me out. Red-faced and panting, she clamped me between her knees, reached for another paper diaper, shook it open, and gift-wrapped me again.

The next morning I sat on an examining table. The embassy doctor said three words: *Lice, Scabies, Worms.* I was full of bugs, ants in my pants.

And that's how I came to America.

# Stalkers

The police call around midnight. "Philoxenia House?"

I know the code word by heart.

"Yes," I reply, "how many?"

"One adult, two kids. Baby needs a crib."

I mentally calculate. The guest room is empty, with a double bed and sleeper sofa, small crib in the corner. Cramped, but warm and safe.

"Okay, I'll let Teresa know they're coming," I say.

"Twenty minutes," the caller says. "An unmarked black pickup." He covers the phone to muffle a yell to someone in the background. Then he's back. "I'm sending a newbie plainclothes man. He'll come the back road through your property because there's been a pileup on 86, but he might miss the turn in the dark." He pauses, then adds, "She has a restraining order, but the husband came back and roughed her up tonight. We're holding him for questioning, but we'll have to release him if she doesn't press charges."

"Tell your driver I'll walk out halfway and guide him in," I say. "Tell him to watch for the light."

"You got it. And thanks. I know it's late, but the other shelters are booked solid."

I shake Tee-tee's arm as she dozes on the couch next to me. "Guests," I say over the laugh track of Friday late-night TV. "A mother and two kids."

Tee-tee's eyelids flutter, then she props herself up on an elbow. "I'm awake, I'm awake," she says groggily.

Her hair is mashed flat on one side, and a crisscross pillow design imprints her cheek. At 58 her *babushka* gray hair is now threaded with strands of white, but she doesn't seem to care. She calls it "aging naturally, like the old silver maple out front," and I've given up on clipping coupons for hair dye and tacking them to the bulletin board, hoping she'll experiment with a

younger look.

Tee-tee lifts the crocheted afghan and swings her legs off the couch. "The caller used the code word, right?" She doesn't wait for me to answer. She knows I know the routine. We've been sheltering women at our house since before I could speak English. Tee-tee—Teresa Tomasio— director of the Helpline Crisis Referral Center by day, undercover shelter director by night, has a soft spot in her heart for women who need to get away but have nowhere to go. We run a safe house called *Philoxenia*—Greek for "love of strangers"—for battered women and their kids. Our county is so large and so rural and so poor that it can't support one secure shelter for every woman who needs safety. Instead we're part of a network of houses scattered in residential neighborhoods, open at a moment's notice. No one would guess just by looking at our two-story Cape Cod that it's a shelter plunked down in the middle of a residential neighborhood. Hidden in plain sight.

The police know where we are. Abusive husbands and boyfriends do not.

We run a tight ship, and here's how it works:

# Τεε-τεε's Rules of hospitality and philoxenia

1. Women are accepted unconditionally. No questions concerning their lifestyle are permitted.

2. We are responsible for what happens to our guests, even meeting with danger ourselves rather than involving the women under our protection.

3. When the time comes, we send the guest safely on her way, making sure she reaches her destination and comes to no harm.

4. The women who stay with us are in no way inferior to us.

5. Nothing is expected in return for our services.

We try our best to follow these rules because we know the consequences if they're broken: Someone gets hurt.

"I'm heading out!" I yell over my shoulder, stepping out the door into a swirl of snowflakes. "I see them coming!"

A gust of bitter wind whips off my parka hood, so I flip it forward again, bunching it with one hand to snug it around my face. The floodlight over the patio door casts a circle of light across the shoveled-off deck planks, diminishing to darkness a few yards beyond. I stare into the blackness of the backyard while glints of snow drift down like ash as the wind cuts back.

I stick out my tongue, and snowdrops melt on contact, cold and sweet, and I swallow, even as a troubling thought flits through my mind: *Acid rain.* During my first New York winters, I thought the best fun in the world was packing a fresh snowball and eating it right off my mitten. Now that I know better, I realize it's like standing behind a bus, snorting up the emissions. A laugh bubbles up from inside me. I'm beginning to think like someone Tee-tee's age, an old woman, scared of everything.

Clouds gape and fold across a rusty-orange gibbous moon revealing half-light one instant, pitch black the next. I switch on my flashlight and trudge across the crusty snow, *crunch,*

*crunch, crunch* with each bootstep. The shadowy limbs of our dwarf apple trees stand nearly naked. Only a scattering of dried leaves cling to branches high up where the deer can't reach, even if they stand on hind legs. My route starts behind the garden and orchard. I crunch over to a wood-slatted fence that runs alongside the back road, extending to the far corner of our property, ending at a state route.

Our back property line lies exactly parallel to Spencer Road, a winding back road that zigzags through the foothills of the Adirondacks. In late winter the wind blasts across our field, leaving only the tops of fence posts poking through the snowdrifts, but now, in November, the ground is frozen, crusted with a topping of snow, a few inches deep at most.

I trace the top slat with my gloved fingertips, then follow the fence, running my palm along the rail as a guide. I fan my light back and forth across the road where autumn rains have turned the drive to mud, and winter has frozen the mud into hard ruts.

Something rustles in the dried needles under the pines. I swing the light toward the sound. A pair of eyes glints in the underbrush, low

to the ground. They disappear for an instant, then flicker back. A dark quick shadow shoots from the bushes and leaps in front of me before crashing through the underbrush on the opposite side. I bite my bottom lip to keep from yelling out. *Only a raccoon, old woman,* I tell myself. *A woodchuck.*

In the distance headlights bounce up and down as a vehicle rocks in and out of shallow ruts as it crosses our property. It slows, then stops, and starts again, as if the driver is unsure of where to go. I swing my flashlight in an arc, the cone of light washing over the pine boughs overhead, dimming, then brightening, the batteries on the verge of conking out. *Just my luck.*

I clunk the flashlight hard on the fence rail hoping to jiggle the battery connections, knock off any corrosion, and give me the satisfaction of bashing something that refuses to obey my command: *Don't die, please don't die.*

I flick it on and off, shake it, and push the thumb switch forward again. It comes on yellow, then dims to ember-orange and flickers once, then cuts out, cloaking me in black. I grip the rail, counting my breaths like a yogi until the clouds gape again and the moon reveals shadowy

silvered forms. I should turn around and head back to the house, replace the batteries, and start out again. It's dangerous in the woods at night, too easy to get lost on our ten-acre property.

But I'm almost there. I flick the switch on and off a few times, bang the light on the rail again. Nothing. I'm ready to pitch the thing into the woods. Without warning, it offers a wavering beam.

The headlights come to a standstill halfway onto our property. "C'mon," I mutter, more to calm myself at hearing a human voice, even if it's only my own, "keep coming this way." I wag the flashlight back-forth, back-forth over my head. The weak beam is barely visible against the thick-needled pine boughs.

The flashlight flickers twice, and dies. I'm swallowed in darkness.

Behind me, the deck light fans across the yard. Up ahead, the headlights dim to parking lights. I stand in the pitch-black middle, like that floaty place between waking and sleeping. Hyper-real, but you can't move a muscle. For a moment I'm paralyzed, not by fear, but by the zombie-like feeling of being thrust into a void. With a whoosh that sucks the breath from me, I

feel a doubling, a sense of being inside my body and floating above myself at the same time, like I've read happens in a near-death experience. Terror seizes me. *Am I dead? Have I died?* I tighten my grip on the fence rail, trying to keep from falling into a mindless panic. The pressure of solid wood reassures me, calms me, and I snap back into myself with a quickness that startles me.

At nearly the same instant, my ears fill with buzzing, as of bees swarming. But how can that be? It's freezing out, the temp's below 30, when bees are logy and disoriented. And then I hear it. Or half-hear it. A voice. A wordless call carried in a gust of wind from deep in the woods. I sense it more than hear it, not my name, but a moaning that pierces my chest, squeezes the soul-nugget within. I strain to hear it again, to prove to myself that it's not just my imagination. It comes again, this time as a sense of water trickling in a shallow creek that never seems to freeze. I'm shivering, but sweating at the same time, like a person possessed.

A branch snaps nearby. Dry leaves crunch under the stand of pines, where the snow hasn't reached the ground. Not the rustle of a squirrel

24

or woodchuck but a heavier thumping sound, of paws or hoofs or boots. I tense, listening for the grunting huff of a bear, the snarl of a bobcat. But the wind picks up, and a low whooshing sweeps through the pinetops.

A trickle of sweat under my breasts snaps me back to reality. I grip the flashlight hard, hoisting it like a weapon. This short distance I can easily cover during daylight recedes into the depths of hell at night. I set my resolve. All I have to do is head toward the parking lights. Then I can catch a ride back.

"Here!" I yell into the dark. "This way!" No answer. They probably can't hear me with the heater on, the windows rolled up tightly against the cold.

I start forward, now able to make out shadowy forms, catlike. One foot forward and down. Then the next. Again and again.

After ten steps forward, with my hand outstretched patting the air in front of me, I step slightly off-balance. I tip sideways, then catch myself. Vertigo washes over me, my heartbeat pulses in my ears. I stand still, listening. The silence is creeping me out. Why aren't the headlights moving? Why doesn't the driver

honk? Announce himself?

An ugly thought seizes my brain.

*Stalking husbands don't announce themselves.*

A searing pain stabs my eyes. I squeeze them shut, gasping from the intensity of the bright light. I drop the flashlight and throw up my hands to shield my eyes.

I'm blinded.

I wave my hands wildly in the air. "Who are you?" I'm scared of what might be coming next. "What do you want?"

"It's a girl," a voice shouts. "Back up. Let's get out of here."

I stumble over an outcropping of rock and grope for my footing. Over I tumble, onto my hip and side.

The spotlight swings off me and lights the bank of pines beside our road. Gears grind as the truck backs up, swings around, jounces over the ruts. Seconds later, the brake lights flare, and the truck fishtails, losing traction and skidding to a stop. The headlights are only a foot from the base of an oak.

The truck backs up, tires spinning, then rumbles down the road into the darkness. It takes the curve fast, sliding, headlights pointed toward the pines. Then it takes a right and guns it down the main road far below.

I push myself onto one elbow. My hip pounds in pain, and a pang shoots along my ribs. I squeeze my eyes shut and fight to regulate my shallow, ragged breathing. I need to get up, get back to the house, and warn Tee-tee. The dot of

deck light behind me swims in a sea of black. Those few hundred yards seem like ten thousand, without a flashlight.

Two pinpricks of light appear at the edge of the property. I crouch low, watching the headlights bounce and weave, heading back up the road straight for me.

It can't be.

*They're back.*

Fear pools at the base of my stomach. I should run back to the house, but I'd never make it without a flashlight. The only thing I can think of is to confront whoever it is head-on. I have the right—it's my property. But I wish I had a weapon more substantial than a plastic flashlight.

I tense my thigh muscles and stand stiffly, shifting from foot to foot to test my hip, in case I need to bolt. The headlights are closer, two blazing eyes rocking up and down with me as their target. I clench my jaw and straighten my shoulders, the way Tee-tee does when she's about to deliver an ultimatum. *Bring it on.*

About ten yards away, the truck motors to a stop, engine idling. Headlights bathe me in bright light. I shield my eyes with my arm.

"You're trespassing," I yell, my words swept away in a gust of wind. I know they can't hear me. But the sound of my own hot-tempered voice braces me for a fight.

The headlights dim to parking lights. A window whirrs as it lowers. The voice is deep and gravelly. "Philoxenia?"

*The code word.* "Yes," I wail in relief.

"State police. I've got your guests."

The door locks pop, and the driver's silhouette reaches across to the passenger side and cracks open the door. In the cab light, two figures cower in the back seat, and a baby mewls like a hungry kitten. Our guests. I pick my way over a rut and steady myself against the truck grille before making my way around the side. A hand extends, and I grab hold and slide into the passenger seat.

"Where's your light, girl? I could have run right over you."

I tap the flashlight on the dash. "Cheap batteries," I say lightly, "generic," pretending as though this is nothing out of the ordinary, something I do every single night of the week. I crane my neck and smile at shadowy faces in the backseat. "Hey, we're almost home."

The driver kicks up the fan, and the air blows hot against the fogged windshield. "Straight ahead?"

"Straight, then veer to the left. I'll show you where." Then casually: "You were here before, right? Then drove off?"

He shakes his head, flicks on his brights, and puts the truck in gear. "Nope. We just got here. Took a little longer than I expected. Traffic's all backed up on 86. A herd of deer got creamed." He glances over at me. "You look a little spooked. Something happen out here?"

I sort through the details, wanting to sound like an objective reporter instead of a blubbering bundle of nerves. "A truck drove up. . . I thought it was you. But they flashed a light at me. Bright, like a spotlight."

"Hunters, probably," the driver says. "Jacking deer."

"Not—?" I lower my voice to a whisper and jerk my thumb toward the back seat.

He gives a quick shake of his head and turns up the radio, drowning out the wailing from the backseat. "Still in custody," he mouths. He steps on the gas, and we slowly pick up speed, heading toward the pinpoint of light in the distance.

I motion toward the cut-off. "Bear left here—"

Out of the depths of darkness, a body plunges into the beam of the headlights.

The driver slams on the brakes. I pitch forward and brace myself against the dashboard. A child shrieks "Mommy!" in the back seat.

A dark, almond-shaped eye stares back at us in terror. With one leap the buck bounds away into the black night.

*The buck springs into the dense thicket, then pauses, flinging up his graceful neck. His large bat-like ears shift in the direction of the engine sounds. He stiffens. But the sounds move away, not toward him. Pawing the ground, he whistles through his nostrils.*

*Her scent lingers, the small human he followed in the darkness. Her scent is sweet, of apple blossoms and honeysuckle. Underneath, the salty smell of fear. She shrieked and screaked*

*like a frightened bobcat. A young one, like his own offspring. She hadn't the stink of larger humans—metallic, sharp, musky. The loud ones tracking through his territory with their smoking sticks.*

*He called to her, and she seemed to hear and sense him, though most humans were unaware of his presence, with their small noses and invisible ears.*

*He chops his hoofs at the frozen ground. The bright light spooked his small doe herd, and they scattered among the trees. Even in his sleep, he is forever fleeing from danger. A great wailing rises in his soul. A congregation of newly departed spirits moan and sigh from the beyond. He has failed his herd, failed to warn them of the danger in crossing the flats where stepping before the speeding light beams means certain death. But how can he fight against human intruders, encroaching, trespassing on his ancestral land, with only antlers and hoofs?*

*He lifts his eyes to the night sky and sends up an angry, silent plea: Help us. Why have you forsaken us? Where is the One who is prophesied to save us?*

*Silence. How foolish he is to believe the old*

*stories. He is their leader, not their savior.*

*The germ of a thought worms its way into his brain, just beyond reach, like an apple on an upper branch. Shaking his rack, he struggles to capture it. Finally it breaks free and surfaces: They need an ally—a human ally, one whose outer weakness disguises inner strength.*

*The scent of apple blossoms floods his nose. The small human. Perhaps she can help. He will ask her tonight.*

# Guests

A toddler and an infant. And the mother doesn't look much older than me. 19? 20 maybe?

She stands in our kitchen, clutching the baby swaddled in a blue blanket to her chest. Her right eye is swollen shut, her nose taped and encrusted with blood. Her arms are hidden by a saggy gray Twin Lakes High sweatshirt—my high school—but they're probably a patchwork of purple-and-blue bruises like those of the other women who come to us in the middle of the night. So young, so scared. I wonder . . . did she fight back? Did she pound him with her fists or dig her nails into his face? If she's like most of the others, she probably just curled in a corner, sobbing, cringing each time his boot kicked her ribs.

It's incomprehensible to me. How could a man who loves a woman beat her up? And how could any woman lay there and take it?

Tee-tee and the driver have a quiet talk near the back door before he hands her a file. She leans against the doorjamb and scans it, sighing heavily, a mixture of weariness and impatience. I know what she's thinking: *Here we go again.* Same old pattern of violence, a never-ending cycle.

I wiggle my fingers and wink at the toddler clinging to her mother's jeans, her mouth plugged with a binkie. She can't be more than two, and the baby looks nearly newborn, a couple months at most. The stink of poopy diaper permeates the kitchen, mixing unappetizingly with the fried fish we had for dinner, and it's obvious the toddler is the culprit from her straining red face and soft grunts.

The driver gives me a two-fingered salute. "Thanks for coming out." He pushes through the door into the mudroom.

"Watch for flying deer," I call after him. My voice startles the baby, and he begins to fuss, his tiny fists beating the air.

Tee-tee follows the driver out and bolts the door behind him. The young mother shivers and presses the baby to her shoulder, jiggling and

shushing. The toddler sinks to the floor and fingers nuggets in the cat's dish, happily curious now that her pants are full.

Tee-tee bustles back into the kitchen, her cheeks red from exertion and the chilly mudroom. "So what was that flying deer comment about, Darya?"

I wave her off. "Private joke. A super-sized buck on our property, that's all. Leaping tall buildings in a single bound."

Tee-tee shifts her gaze toward the mother and pastes on a welcoming smile. She glances down at the file in her hand, then steps forward. "Libby, welcome. I'm Teresa. Please call me Tee-tee." She points to me. "And this is my daughter, Darya." Tee-tee crouches next to the toddler who is busily chewing cat kibble. "And who is this?" Tee-tee sniffs the air and crinkles her nose.

The small girl swivels and buries her face between her mother's legs.

"Maddie," her mother rasps between swollen lips, the lower one split open like a grilled sausage. "And Ethan." She tips her chin at the infant, now cooing.

"Well, Maddie, would you like a juice box?" Tee-tee stands and reaches into the cupboard over the microwave. "And some cookies?"

Maddie peeks from behind her mother's legs.

She leans forward and spits out kibble chunks on the floor, then inches toward Tee-tee, one hand still grasping her mother's jeans, the other reaching for treats.

Tee-tee strips the cellophane wrapper off the straw and punctures the juice box. "Let's all go upstairs and get ready for bed," she orders cheerily. Turning to me, she mouths, "Lock the front door. And run a bath."

I pick up the brown shopping bag that holds a jumble of clothes, disposable diapers, and a few plushie toys. With Tee-tee leading the way, we climb the stairs to the guest room. My hip screams on the first few treads, then settles into a dull ache. Nikky's bedroom is silent, door closed. Ten-year-olds, it seems, are comatose when they hit the bed and can sleep through anything, including nuclear disasters, terrorist attacks, midnight phone calls, and battered wives with fussy babies who drop in any time of night.

As we pad down the hallway, Libby stops dead. She sways, and I reach for her arm. "I need a bathroom," she whispers in a shaky voice.

Tee-tee scoops Ethan out of her arms, and I hustle Libby into the bathroom. Dropping to her knees, she bends over and vomits into the toilet, a mucousy yellow issue with little substance. I wet a washcloth and press it to her forehead as

she dry heaves.

"It's okay, you're okay," I soothe, rubbing her back.

She gives me a weak, lopsided smile. "Must be something I ate."

"Must be," I say, knowing full well it was a fist sandwich.

We follow the same routine as with all our nighttime guests: bathing, diapering, snacking, bedding, dosing with aspirin. Tee-tee assures Libby that she and the children are safe, that no one knows of this place except the police and Social Services.

"And no phone calls to your husband," Tee-tee admonishes, "or to any relatives. We don't want anyone tracing a call back to this address. Is that understood?"

Libby nods from her pillow. Maddie is snuggled next to her, eyelids fluttering in half-sleep, sucking her binkie, stroking a small pink blankie against her cheek. Ethan snores softly in the crib.

"Sleep tight," Tee-tee whispers, dragging the comforter up over Libby's shoulders. "Don't let the bedbugs bite."

This is Tee-tee's stock bedtime sign-off, and I always wonder what our guests think of it. With all the bashing and battering they've just been

through, biting bedbugs are probably the least of their worries.

I lie awake, listening to Tee-tee snore and replaying my freak-out in the woods. I'm not usually a drama queen. I'm more of the cool-cucumber type, pragmatic and calm under pressure. No tear-shedding for me. While Tee-tee's blubbering into her hankie over a sentimental Hallmark movie, I'm more likely to be smooshing my face into a pillow to keep from laughing. So why am I suddenly a roiling pot of hysterics? It's aggravating, like stubbing a toe or getting a paper cut, a small annoyance with a big pain factor.

A child coughs wetly, and the floorboards squeak as Libby crosses to the bathroom. The toilet flushes. And with it I flow down the black hole of sleep.

I don't know how long I've been asleep when I hear it.

An explosion. Shattering glass. Downstairs.

My eyes snap open. I jerk up onto my elbows, holding my breath, listening in the dark silence. Muffled staccato thuds, then a low whooshing sound.

I throw back the covers and hit the floor. The floorboards squeak as Tee-tee scuffs down the

hall in her slippers. She flings open my door.

"Call 911." Tee-tee's silhouette grips a baseball bat. "Check Nikky, and warn Libby. And all of you stay upstairs."

I'm scrabbling on the nightstand for my cell when it hits me—it's on the kitchen counter.

Tee-tee is already descending the stairs as I step into the hall, lit only by a hooded nightlight. Nikky's door is still closed. I rap instead on Libby's door and try the knob. Locked. But Maddie is whimpering, so I know they're awake.

"Stay put," I hiss at the door. "Don't come out."

"Out. Get out," Tee-tee screams from below.

I hear a loud whack, then a bellowing. It's the moment I've imagined, and dreaded. *The husband. He's found us.*

Armed with nothing, I creep downstairs, feeling my way in the dark, the pain in my hip obliterated by fear.

Tee-tee's voice is loud and threatening. "Out! Out NOW."

A loud whistle and snort answer her back.

I round the corner and stop dead in my tracks. He stands motionless in the corner of the shadowy room, lit only by the twinkle lights on our Christmas tree, which now lays toppled, the

top boughs brushing the brick of the fireplace.
Glass shards from the shattered patio door litter
the carpet.

Not Libby's stalking, hotheaded husband.
Not a spouse bent on revenge.

Our intruder is a magnificent, terrified
deer.

The buck quivers, his flanks gashed and
bleeding. Blood drips from his distended nostrils.
A wild gleam fills his eyes. With a shake of his
head, he paws the carpet, glass crunching with
every thump. He lowers his huge forked rack

and strikes the floor lamp. It teeters and crashes against the metal fireplace screen.

Tee-tee catches sight of me. She wields the bat over her shoulder, ready to swing. Her arms tremble from the weight. "Get a broom and help me move this stupid beast," she orders in a shaky voice, one I've never heard before. She's scared, as scared as I was tonight out in the woods.

I inch forward, keeping my arms at my sides, my muscles tense and ready to bolt, disobeying Tee-tee for the first time in my life. A small shard of glass pierces my bare heel, and I bite my lip to keep from crying out.

The buck flinches, as if he feels my pain. As I approach he looks me straight in the eye. For a long moment we lock eyes in the glow of the tree lights, not moving. Whorls of brown fur contour his face. His tail flicks once. A whiff of rankness assaults my nose—blood, dung, muck. I should be scared, but I'm not. Not at all.

Tee-tee's warning voice drones in my head. She tugs at my nightshirt, but I shrug her off. After a moment's hesitation I extend my hand, just a bit.

"Hello," I say, low and friendly. "I'm Darya."

The buck's ears shoot forward. He takes one step toward me, sniffs, catches my scent. His black eyes pierce through me with the shininess of

the enchanted. The walls seem to swell outward, everything curved as in a TV cartoon, and then shrink inward, pressing against the two of us. I nearly drown in those dark liquid pools.

Emboldened, I pluck an apple from the fruit bowl on the coffee table. I keep prattling softly, as I used to do with Nikky when he was cranky from teething. "Hello," I murmur again. "Are you hungry?" I offer the apple to him on my palm. "You like apples, don't you? Go ahead, take it."

The buck's ears twitch. He turns his massive head toward me, shudders, and nervously thumps the carpet again, shaking his crest, whistling through his nostrils. His sad, almond-shaped eyes leak fluid, like tears. Deer tears.

Then I hear it again, the buzzing swarm with no bees. I dig my nails into my palms to ground me and prevent me from splitting in two, both me-entities swept into a formless abyss. An icy wind whooshes through the smashed door and, with it, the voice that is no voice, like the reverberation of canyon echo. What is it trying to tell me? What does it need? The apple drops from my hand as the room shifts and swirls, pitching me into a cavern with a moss-patched rockface, silent except for the *plink-plink-plink* of dripping water.

Tee-tee hisses at me. "Stop it, Darya. Are

you crazy?"

I shake my head, more to snap me out of my reverie. "It's okay, he won't hurt us," I whisper, not knowing why or how I'm certain of this.

The buck pricks his ears forward, then backward. I take a small step to the right on the ball of my foot, keeping my weight off my punctured heel. Slowly I lift my hand toward him and click my tongue. He doesn't flinch. Only an ear twitches. He's all muscle and rack, with the strength to gore me or crush me under his hoofs.

What am I trying to do? Pet him? This *is* crazy, and logically even *I* know it. I've read reports of trainers being killed by so-called tame animals. Placid tigers mauling visiting guests. House-bred chimpanzees raised like human children, viciously turning on their owners. But he doesn't seem dangerous, not like a charging bull or snapping crocodile. Sure, he's scared. I can see that. But this beast exudes dignity and arrogance, obvious from the noble way he holds his head and stares straight at me. I'm enamored. And something more, something I can't label. It's as though I've run across an old friend, one who's been absent for a long time and has now reappeared in a happy homecoming.

Tee-tee inches back and picks up the portable

phone. Three clicks as she punches 911, then a whispery "We need help here."

The mantel clock chimes three, loud clanging *boings* that normally would be background noise. But here in the tense silence, they resound like Big Ben. Before I can move again, a ball of fur shoots across my feet so swiftly and suddenly that I flinch. Our old tabby leaps atop the couch, spitting, arch-backed as her claws dig into the upholstery. She *yeowl*s once, then streaks out of the room in a blur of tawny fur.

Startled, the buck rears on his muscled haunches, showing his snow-white underbelly. With a snort and shake of his head, he whirls and leaps through the gaping hole in what was once our patio door, now only a frame edged with glass shards.

Tee-tee drops the bat and collapses on the sofa. "Will this night ever end?" she moans, head in hands. "What else could possibly happen to us? Am I dreaming? Tell me this is just a nightmare."

I hobble over and stand behind her. I rub her shoulders, and she groans from the relief my kneading fingers bring her. My sleep shirt is spattered with blood, but she rests her head against me and exhales a deep breath. A siren wails, coming closer.

Finally Tee-tee opens her eyes and surveys the damage. "At least it wasn't Libby's husband."

"You'd better tell her." I pick up a lamp at my feet and replace it on an end table. I snap the lamp on, and the room appears in its true form—a shambles. "She's probably out on the roof by now." I limp to the ottoman and sit, foot up, examining the thin spear of glass impaled in my bloody heel. Before I can talk myself out of it, I pinch the shard between my fingers and yank it out. I wipe my bloody fingers across my nightshirt, merging blood, the buck's and my own. The thought makes me smile.

Tee-tee takes my foot into her lap. She squints at the wound. "Lord, I'm blind without my bifocals. Stay right here. I'll get the first aid kit, and check on the folks upstairs."

Tee-tee props my foot on the cushion and leaves in a swirl of pink bathrobe. Slippers softly clump up the stairs. Libby's sharp cry, then Tee-tee's voice comforting her. Nikky is blissfully silent.

Cold wind blows through the gaping hole in the door. Fine snow drifts across the doorjamb. I shiver, but from excitement, not cold. The siren dies as it nears our driveway. Flashing lights strobe through the windows.

I hum to myself.

He'll be back. I know it. I feel it.
He's told me so.

*The buck stands in the pine forest, staring at the lit doorway. His hocks quiver, and sharp points of pain jab his back where shards of glass stick. He tests the air with his sensitive nose. No danger.*

*He had followed her tracks, retracing her boot prints running along the fence, back to her home. Fooled by his reflection, like a newborn fawn peering into a pond, he thought another buck approached, so he charged. Instead of clashing with his foe, he met solid resistance, followed by a cracking, sharp points penetrating his back, and a human squawking like a crow.*

*Then she appeared, the sweet-smelling girl whose voice sounded like a small animal's. Twice in the last week, he had been chased by humans with lights and metal sticks—but this human was different. She posed no threat. Instead, she offered food.*

*Is she the ancient prophecy come true?*

*And she has a name:* Dar-Ya. *He will call her again, using her name, and perhaps she will understand.*

*He springs to the right, then left, through the woods. He will tell the herd.*

## Libby's Lament

Beware
of young men
who stand at your door
stealing your kisses
and begging for more
delivering roses
a fistful of roses

He was an athlete
who asked me to dance
flirty and handsome
exuding romance
he promised true love
I surrendered my heart
a bond forged in fire
till death do us part
with tender caresses
words gentle as spring
he offered me
a wedding ring
clenched in his fist
a wedding ring

he cut off my friends
he blackened my eye
I threatened to leave
he snarled, "You will die."

Beware
of young men
who make you their slave
then beat you and kick you
and dance on your grave
delivering punches
a fistful of punches

He promised to change
I deadened my heart
a bond scorched by fire
in life we must part

Beware
of young men
with words soft and sweet
who beg for forgiveness
and weep at your feet
delivering lies
a mouthful of lies

# santa's here

Libby is nursing the baby at the breakfast table. Ethan startles when I shuffle past in my slippers and fusses until he latches on again. Maddie sits in Nikky's old highchair, marching a plastic dinosaur through the milk in her cereal bowl. I avert my eyes to give Libby some privacy and busy myself at the counter, spooning hazelnut coffee into the coffeemaker filter. I know it's natural and healthy, and women have been breastfeeding since God made bosoms, but I feel as if I've walked in on someone naked. I look down at my nightshirt. Flat.

My day is weirdly complete: Deer at the door and boobs at the breakfast bar.

"Coffee, Libby?" I whisper, trying not to clank

the mugs in the drainboard and disturb Ethan's blissful guzzling.

"Sure," Libby croaks. "Thanks."

I drape a dishtowel over her shoulder to use as a burp cloth.

Ethan's eyes pop open for an instant. He pats the white orb of her breast and grins. She is his mother, and he recognizes and loves her, even though her face is beaten to a pulp. I'm filled with a sudden, strange thought: *That's what it's like to have a real mother.*

I peel and slice a banana, the house silent, except for a wet sucking sound and the soft *bloop-bloop-bloop* of Maddie's dinosaur as it smooshes through the primordial ooze of soggy cereal. Libby's breast milk smells sweet and grassy. She leans back with a contented look, humming, as if she were sunning on a tropical island, not hiding from an abusive husband.

Did my mother nurse me? I can't remember. Nikky was a bottle baby—adoptive mothers simply can't perform some birth mother functions, no matter how much they'd like to.

After the coffeemaker drips and hisses, I fill a mug, carry it to the table, and place it near her free hand, looking everywhere but at her chest. "You're totally safe here," I whisper, "and you

can stay as long as you like."

Libby tries to smile, but it comes out more of a grimace. She looks worse. She's tried to cover the bruises with tinted makeup and powder, but the effect is clownish and streaky. Her nose looks as if it's been dredged in flour.

"Can I get you some aspirin?"

She shakes her head and winces. "Not good for the baby." She runs her fingers lightly over Ethan's fine hair. Her good eye stares at me. "So it was only a deer," she says. Ethan's head drops away, his mouth rimmed with milk. As he snoozes, his little lips purse and smack as though he's still nursing.

"A disoriented deer," I say lightly. "Forgot to program his GPS." I shift sideways to sneak a peek at the brown rectangle of patio door, a patchwork of cardboard duct-taped to the frame, thanks to firefighters decked out in shiny black boots and baggy bunker pants, portable radios squawking, who'd responded to Tee-tee's call. The fire department, they told us, was responsible for residence "critter calls"—usually for treed kittens or bedroom bats—never deer. Wildlife conservation handled deer control and injuries. The DPW hauled off rotting carcasses. Since our deer-in-the-house call didn't fit any department's jurisdiction, the response time

lagged. They crunched over the busted glass, checked electrical wiring, cracked jokes. But even though they'd come too late, Tee-tee was never one to waste free manpower. Five minutes later two brawny firefighters were slitting cardboard boxes and slapping up duct-tape while Tee-tee supervised in her bathrobe.

I turn back to Libby and pump her with encouraging words. "No one knows about this place except the police. You're safe here. You'll stay for a while, won't you?" My eyes drift to the blue bruises on her chest. Nursing mother as punching bag.

Libby shrugs. "They want me to press charges." She clips her bra cup and lifts Ethan to her shoulder for a burp. "They can't hold him unless I press charges."

"But you're going to, right? You're not going to let him get away—"

"I made a vow, for better or worse. This is the worse, I guess."

I press on, gently. "He'll do it again, Libby. They always do." I try to keep my voice calm. "You'll be back in less than a month, I guarantee it."

Libby gives me her weak, lopsided smile. "What do you know—you're just a kid."

I don't try to explain that I've seen more

dysfunctional relationships in the past ten years—more fragile, broken women cowering in fear—than she'll experience in a lifetime. Women who take beatings from guys and then blame themselves. I bite my tongue to keep from giving Libby a bit of advice from "just a kid" like me: *Cut your losses and bail, girl.*

Maddie bounces up and down in her chair, squealing. "Santa! Mommy, look. Santa's here."

"Not yet, honey," Libby says, reaching out a hand and straightening Maddie's bib. "It's not Christmas yet. Not for a long time."

Maddie flings her spoon, clattering it across the table. She struggles to free herself from the highchair strap, her chubby hands shoving against the tray. "Santa, Mommy!" She raises a hand and points behind me.

I swivel in the direction of her finger and catch the top of a brown head as it ducks beneath the window.

*Libby's husband. He's found us.*

My chair scrapes as I shove back from the table. Coffee sloshes out of mugs, silverware clatters against plates.

"Libby, hide." I unclip Maddie's chair belt and pluck her out, then drop to a crouch beneath the kitchen cabinets where we can't easily be seen. Maddie squeals and clutches my neck in

a death grip, her legs locked around my waist. Ethan howls as Libby slides down to crouch under the table.

"Mommy, Mommy, Mommy," Maddie whimpers into my hair.

"Shhh," I murmur in Maddie's ear. "Shhh." I bounce and shush, sneaking glances at the window. Water runs upstairs. Tee-tee's singing arias in the shower, so no help there. The kitchen phone is, in reality, a mere three quick steps away. But considering I'd be as exposed as a deer in the headlights, it might as well be in the next galaxy.

The brown head pops up again. Calm dark eyes survey inside, jaw moving in a chewing motion.

Relief explodes in my chest. I whoop and fall backward on the floor with Maddie in my arms. She lets out a squeal as I squeeze her to my chest and tickle her sides.

Libby cautiously peeks from under the table. "Darya? What's going on?"

I hoist Maddie to my hip, help Libby up, and draw her to the window. "Maddie's right. Santa *is* here."

A lone doe stands in our raised kitchen garden, foraging for leftover herbs and late-season squash. Her tail flicks from side to side

in an unhurried beat.

"Santa!" Maddie yells. She kicks her legs and wriggles against me. "Down. Me want down."

The doe stiffens and perks her ears forward as if she can hear us. In one swift leap she bounds from the bricked-in garden and across the graveled drive, heading for the tree line. Her tail flashes a white *V* through the pines.

"Rudolph," Maddie wails. "Come back."

Nikky shuffles into the kitchen, yawning and scratching his bare chest, dotted with a sprinkle of fine light hairs. My baby brother is growing up. "Hey," he says, perking up at the sight of visitors. "What's all the noise about?"

I wink at Libby. "Refugee from the North Pole." I shift Maddie to my hip and wrap an arm around him, leaning in to kiss his forehead, nearly on a level with my own. "Checking to see if you've been naughty or nice."

*The doe bounds into the woods to join her sisters. She snorts, full of joy. She has found the young human her mate spoke of, the Dar-Ya,*

*safe inside her enclosure, holding a tiny fawn-sized human with a similar snout and hair. They seemed glad to see her, their eyes bright, their voices high with squeals.*

*Although the yard smells foul, of blood and human scent, the doe knows she has nothing to fear. She will tell the others, and perhaps they will all return.*

*Dar-Ya will certainly bring food, as promised by the ancestors.*

"Let's get to work," Tee-tee says, handing me a broom and dustpan. "There's glass to be swept and blood to be scrubbed."

"What about Nikky?" I turn just in time to catch him rounding the banister and fleeing upstairs. "Can't he help too?"

Tee-tee gapes at me, as if I'd suggested that Nikky join the Marines. "Don't be ridiculous, Darya. He's far too young to handle broken glass. He might cut himself."

But, of course, it's of no concern to her if *I* puncture my arteries and bleed to death.

"Start over here," she says, pointing to a corner near the fireplace. "Get the big shards first, then we'll vacuum up the splinters. Nikky's always walking around with bare feet, and I can't have my baby boy hurt."

My punctured heel throbs at the thought. I wait for her to ask about it. She doesn't.

I dig the broom bristles into the corner and drag glass toward me, then slide the shards into the dustpan. Tee-tee hums as she flexes open the stepladder and positions it near the patio door opening. I decide now's a good time to tell her about my run-in with the first truck, leaving out the part where I freaked out. I don't want to be caught up in a lie in case the officer last night mentioned it. Besides I'm curious to know her take on what happened.

"It's those hunters illegally jacking deer on our property." Tee-tee's up on the stepladder tacking a wide swath of heavy plastic sheeting over the cardboard-patched door. "Shining a spotlight on deer to freeze them in place."

"But what's the point? I thought hunters wanted to kill deer, not scare them."

"It makes them easier to shoot. A deer frozen in a spotlight is an easy target for a hunter firing a high-powered rifle."

Or *me* frozen in the spotlight. I could have

60

been shot last night. The thought makes me shudder. "I thought hunting at night was against the law."

"It is, but deer are most active at night—that's when they feel safest. Hunters flush out places where deer feed, driving them onto lands that aren't posted."

"That's not fair!" Glass shards clatter as I toss them into an empty paint can.

"Deer aren't armed. They can't defend themselves. And our land is posted for *No Hunting*, right?"

"I've tacked those yellow signs to every damn tree bordering our property, Darya."

The blood spots on the rug and hardwood floor have darkened. I lick a finger and bend to touch one of the clotted drops. It stains my finger the color of Tee-tee's port wine. "Why do you think the buck smashed through our door?"

"Jacking makes deer skittish, jumpy. The buck might have seen its reflection in the glass and charged it, thinking it was another buck. Deer get aggressive when they're in rut."

"He was bleeding." I hand her the shears. "And he was crying."

"Not tears," Tee-tee says, scissoring her way from top to bottom. "It's just an oily secretion from the ducts near their eyes."

"But he *could* have been crying," I insist. "Maybe animals cry, but they don't want us to know they're crying. They can't make crying sounds, so they just look sad, with weepy eyes."

Tee-tee stands back to study her tape job, hands on hips. "Good enough until we can get to the Home Fix-it store." A stiff wind buffets the house, rattling the cardboard, making the plastic whistle. She fans herself with a square of cardboard. "Lord, is it hot in here or is it just me?"

Here it comes. She's having one of her hot flashes. Sweat glistens above her lip, her face turns a fiery red. She flaps her sweater like a bird on take-off, then cracks open the patio door to let in some icy air. As though it isn't cold enough in here with no insulating glass. Last week when we watched a special on global warming, Tee-tee insisted she knew the cause: Thousands of menopausal women having hot flashes at the same time.

Hot flashes turn her into Her Royal Crankiness. And anger seems to trigger them. Her eyebrows gather like thunderclouds ahead of a storm. She's about to launch into me, I'm sure of it.

"What on earth possessed you to approach that buck? I specifically told you to stay

upstairs." She shakes a finger at me. "You could have been hurt—or killed. Wild animals are unpredictable."

I shrug, and check the impulse to blurt out the truth, that I think the buck communicated with me as though we were old friends. Instead I say lightly, "He had me at hello."

Tee-tee heaves a sigh. "Be serious, Darya."

"Okay, he was wounded and tangled in the tree, and I figured he wouldn't charge if I moved slowly and kept my voice soft. Like that crocodile hunter guy on TV always did."

Tee-tee slides back the patio door as far as possible with its patchwork of cardboard and plastic. "Don't forget, he *died* from an animal wound."

I don't bother with a rebuttal. When Tee-tee chooses to be obstinate, arguing with her is hopeless. I can disagree with her all I want, but she always has the last word.

We don heavy leather work gloves and haul the mauled Christmas tree, stripped of its bulbs and lights, over the threshold and across the blood-spattered deck. A trail of hoof prints ends at the woods' edge, and red droplets dot the snow. A trail so evident that even the clumsiest hunter couldn't fail to read the message: *Wounded deer here.* Our tree leaves its own trail of green

needles as we lug it to its dumping place near the edge of the field.

A glint of gold catches my eye. I reach through the prickly branches and pluck out my third-grade Christmas ornament, a brown reindeer with clothespin ears, plastic googly-eyes, and a red felt bowtie. I slip it into my pocket. At least I've rescued one deer.

Tee-tee lifts the trunk end of the tree and gives it one final pitch into the field. A stubble of harvested cornstalks pokes up through a light snow cover. "The town's deer culling plan has brought this on, I'm afraid. It's going to draw hunters from all over the state, and out of state. And not everyone knows—or obeys—the law."

D. E. E. R. The Deer Early Extermination Resolution, passed by the town board of trustees at last week's meeting. The local newscast reported that D. E. E. R. had been voted in unanimously to temporarily eliminate the state restrictions on the number of deer that could be taken by each hunter. Hunters could kill as many deer as they wanted to cut back the growing deer population.

Shotgun season started last week. Distant booms woke me at sunrise. Hunters came to stalk deer, orange-vested, camouflaged men who worked in city offices during the year, crept

through the woods with deer tags dangling from their hips. Jumpy and hyped up, they shot at everything that moved, sometimes even their buddies.

"You stick close to home from now on," Tee-tee warns me. "I'll check with the state police barracks and the DEC tomorrow to see if they can't send out an extra patrol at night. If the jackers are caught, they'll get a fine and up to a year in jail."

At the edge of our woods, we choose a chest-high, bushy-needled Scotch pine, one we can easily drag into the house and decorate with our remaining bulbs. Armed with a hacksaw, I lie on my belly and trim a few lower branches, then cut a gash across the main trunk. The gash weeps a tear of clear aromatic resin. I stop sawing. *Is the tree crying?*

A bough moves aside, and Tee-tee's face appears above me, framed by green needles. "What's wrong? Is the blade too dull?"

"Maybe we should buy an artificial tree this year."

Tee-tee huffs a reply. "Fat chance. No fakes when we own ten acres of the real thing." The boughs spring back into place, but a boot nudges my leg. "Keep sawing, girl."

"I'm not your slave," I mutter, shifting my

weight to get a tighter grip on the saw, the saw Nikky should be wielding, not me. Heaven forbid he injure his precious pinkies. I order my arm to obey, reminding myself how much Tee-tee likes to decorate the house before Thanksgiving. She says the twinkle lights and pine-scented candles make her feel festive. Her work at the Helpline is more depressing during the holidays, as she's swamped with calls from folks needing food, shelter, cash, or a nonjudgmental ear. Tee-tee sees a lot of hungry people and sad people and lonely people. That's why I know there's so much misery in the world. I wouldn't have believed it otherwise. The holidays morph Tee-tee into a Type-E Personality: doing Everything for Everybody Every day. Maybe it's the lack of daylight, she says, or the stress from maxing out their credit cards as they frantically buy gifts they can't afford for relatives who only re-gift them anyway, that makes people feel like flushed deer, skittish and jumpy.

With a soft whoosh, the tree topples.

"I'll take the trunk, you guide the top," Tee-tee tells me. We slide the tree toward the door, and I swivel to lift the top boughs.

"I've been thinking about signing up for Driver's Ed." I try to say it casually, as if the idea just popped into my head, and I hadn't been

thinking about it nearly every minute since I turned sixteen, but my heart is racing beneath my voice. "But that's only offered during the summer, and they might cut it for lack of funding. So maybe you could take me out now that I have my permit."

Tee-tee harrumphs and glares at me. She hates the idea of me driving.

"I could help out with the shopping—"

"Lord Almighty!" Tee-tee roars. She drops the pine trunk and storms off the deck. "Shoo." She flicks her work gloves overhead. "Move it, you greedy deer. Take a hike."

The herd freezes. A buck and three does stare at us for several seconds, then continue lazily chewing. One doe approaches the bird feeder, rises on her hind legs, and nibbles seed from the plastic tray.

Tee-tee is red-faced. Her voice ratchets up an octave. "Scram, deer." She strides forward, furious now. "Beat it." She hurls her gloves at the herd. "Don't just stand there, Darya. Help me. Bang on something."

The buck snorts his defiance, striding forward to a stiff-legged stance. The cuts on his flanks are caked with dried blood.

He stares right at me.

My legs are jittery, unstable. Everything

seems to be running in slow motion. I can't look away, and I don't really want to. Tee-tee's voice fades, replaced by the sound of blood thudding in my ears. I seem to be caught in a limbo between two worlds, one wild, one human. I'm paralyzed, unable to exist in either. I swallow hard, hoping my ears will pop. Anything to bring me back to reality.

*Clang-clang-clang.*

Nikky stands by the back door, banging on a saucepan with a metal spoon.

Startled, the deer crouch, rigid. Tee-tee moves toward the apple orchard, and their black eyes follow her.

*Clang-clang-clang.* Nikky steps out into the yard, his spoon beating out a staccato. His mouth is stretched in a mile-wide grin. He's clearly enjoying his role as game warden.

The buck steps pluckily toward us, tail swishing, tilting his fine head and regarding me with a sideways eye, a bold fellow. The does raise their black lips and snort, their hindquarters jiggling in a rhythmic dance. Some unnamable tenderness bubbles up inside me, and a giggle nearly bursts from my mouth. Here we are, one big happy family serenaded by kitchen utensils.

Tee-tee bends and pockets a couple of frozen, shriveled brown apples, and marches toward the

herd. She whips one at the herd, then another, missing both times. "Get," she screeches at them over Nikky's banging. "Get out."

With a twitch of an ear, the buck swivels on his hindquarters and leaps gracefully toward the woods. As if on cue the does bound behind him.

The banging stops mid-clang. Nikky raises his instruments in triumph. "Please, please, hold your applause," he says, making little bows in our direction.

Flapping her sweater, Tee-tee slogs wordlessly across the snow toward the mudroom. The back door slams. Then a string of curse words.

Now's obviously not the time to beg for a driving lesson.

*The buck plunges into the piney growth. He follows his does deeper into the woods, then stops and turns toward the house. He saw her again, the young human. She stood in the opening near the invisible barrier, the solid one he had crashed through.*

*Her scent was overpowered by the burning-flesh reek of the large human who squawked at them like an enraged crow. But the young human's eyes showed a tinge of fright, then amusement mixed with curiosity, as his son's eyes did when a hunter approached the herd.*

*She held his eyes like a bobcat ready to pounce, but he sensed no danger. Instead, she seemed akin to him, not in body, but in spirit. And not of this place, but of somewhere distant. Yes, she is a stranger too.*

*He tried to call to her. Had she heard? He will try again, when their paths merge.*

# The name trapped inside

I'm a worrier. It's my nature. Global warming. Nuclear war. Alien abductions. Paper or plastic.

For a long time I worried I'd be sent away, but Tee-tee assured me over and over that this adoption wasn't temporary—it was forever. But I'd read about adopted kids getting foisted back on agencies and orphanages and foster homes. Given one-way flights back to a homeland whose language they no longer speak, like humans raised on Mars, then returned to Earth. The adoption business seemed to rank with pest control and flood prevention—no guarantees of success and every chance for failure.

I once asked Tee-tee if she knew what had

happened to my parents, and she said, "No, not really." The orphanage records were sealed by the court. She couldn't quite understand the director, even though a translator was present. His English was rough and mostly one-syllable. "Gone," he'd said about my mother, crossing himself in the Orthodox fashion. When asked about my father, he'd simply sneered, fished a handkerchief from his back pocket, and honked into it. A blessed saintly mother. A cursed father, worth no more than snot in a rag.

I've spent a big chunk of my life convinced that I was on Tee-tee's short list of targets. After all, I'm the incidental child, excess baggage, the one who came with the real prize—baby Nikky. I can understand why she took me on even though it cramped her lifestyle. What choice did she have? To spend the rest of her life knowing she'd broken up our family, separated brother and sister? So she caved and did the right thing, even though it's been a hardship for her—a single, older woman raising two kids.

*Mommy.* I never call Tee-tee by that name, but Nikky does, because he can't remember our real mother. I look at it this way: My birth mother died. Tee-tee is my substitute mother, like a substitute teacher at school who fills in temporarily for the real teacher. To me, she's a

warm and friendly set of initials: T. T.

She's good with that now, but in the beginning she felt hurt. Tee-tee scared me, and so did her house. I wasn't always a scaredy-cat. At the orphanage I could stomp any kid who stole my chewing gum. But when I stepped into Tee-tee's house, I was immersed in a strangeness that made my teeth chatter.

*Where are the others?* I asked, although Tee-tee couldn't understand my words. I clambered up the stairs and stumbled from room to room searching for more adults and other kids. Tee-tee puffed behind me, weighed down by Nikky drowsing on her shoulder, his head bobbing. At the third bedroom she laid Nikky in a large wooden-rail crib. A mobile of glittery sea creatures dangled over his head.

Tee-tee grasped my hand, but I shrieked and wrestled away, thrashing, kicking at her shins. *Nyet! Nyet!* I howled at her, along with hate-filled words she couldn't understand but read from my body language: *Don't touch me, you old witch*. Her face crumpled suddenly, the hard lines softening. She pointed to Nikky snoozing in the crib, then put the finger to her lips and made a shushing sound. She stepped backward and swept a hand toward the door, motioning me to follow her. I crept behind her down the

hall, keeping an arm's-length away in case she tried to grab me. She stopped at a door, turned, and winked at me. She stepped back so I could peek inside. The high bed was topped with a white down comforter as fluffy as any cloud I'd seen from the plane. Before I could resist she reached out and tapped my chest, then folded her hands against her cheek and pretended to sleep. I pointed at her, then myself. *You and me?* She shook her head. She tapped my chest again, then swept an arm to circle the room. All at once my teeth began chattering, and I bit down hard to make them stop. An entire bedroom all to myself?

But where did the others sleep? In our Moscow flat I shared a room with my parents, sleeping on a cot under the window. My grandparents slept on a pullout sofa in the dining room. My uncle spread a mat on the kitchen floor after dinner.

I shared my orphanage room with eight others. I'd never in my life slept alone.

Or ate a whole bowl of strawberries.

Or watched cartoons.

Or listened to music through earphones.

It scared me, yes. But I tasted freedom and yearned for more. I plunged into American culture like a Bolshoi ballerina gliding through the air in a grand jete and landing to a standing

ovation. In two weeks I had a basic grasp of simple English words, picking up new ones every day from TV shows. Tee-tee cracked up when I pointed at her and said, "Looney Tunes." She wiped away a tear when I hugged Nikky and crooned, "Love you, beebee."

I know she waited and waited. But I couldn't say the one word she wanted to hear: *Mommy*.

# Damn Deer

I climb the stairs to the guest room. I knock and call Libby's name. No one answers, so I call her name again. I open the door a crack.

The blinds are closed, the lights off. My eyes take a minute to adjust to the dark.

"I should never have come." Libby sits cross-legged on her unmade bed, hands folded in her lap. Clothes litter the floor. Wadded diapers are heaped on top of the dresser.

"Love what you've done with the place," I say in a feeble attempt at lightening the gloom. I snap on a small bedside lamp and place a plastic dollhouse on the rug, one that Tee-tee saved from my first American Christmas.

Maddie squeals, clapping her hands in

delight. Ethan jerks awake in his crib, then settles back down with a baby sigh, making tiny kissing motions with his mouth.

"This was a mistake," Libby continues. "I need to go home."

For a long moment I say nothing. I had a feeling this might be coming.

Wincing, Libby stiffly lifts herself off the bed and starts stuffing clothes into the shopping bag. Her hair is wet and lank from a shower, her makeup gone. Her bruises have turned from black to yellow. She looks younger than me now, maybe ten, about Nikky's age. But she's thinking like a two-year-old.

"I know you think it's over," I begin, keeping my voice calm, "but you might be wrong."

I crouch next to Maddie and help her sort plastic furniture into small rooms. *Bam! Bam! Bam!* Maddie bashes the girl doll with the boy doll. "Bad mommy," she growls, but then seems puzzled. She throws down the doll, leaps up, and wraps her arms around Libby's legs. "Daddy gave Mommy boo-boos."

Libby runs a hand over her daughter's head.

"Do you want something to eat?" I ask.

"Thanks . . . no."

"Maybe I should go," I say, rising to my feet.

"No, wait!" She stands staring at me, seemingly unsure of what to say next. "Are. . . are you in school?"

"Yeah. A junior at Twin Lakes High."

Her eyes brighten. "Great school, Twin Lakes. I was in school. At Fillmore Community College. Pre-med.

"Before you had kids, right?"

Libby sighs. "I had to drop out." She pauses, and I wonder what's running through her head, why her plans changed. "But I plan to go back." Her tone is defiant.

"So why not stay here a few days until things calm down? Until you get your head together?"

"I can't stay here for days," she says, folding a white onesie. "We can't barge in on you and your mother and brother."

"Sure you can. It's what we do. We take in"—*beat-up women like you*, I almost say—"guests all the time. And don't worry about barging in on our family." My mouth runs on autopilot. "Because Tee-tee's not our real mother. She adopted us." *Stupid.* What possessed me to blurt that out?

"Oh." A look of concern crosses Libby's face, and she squeezes my shoulder. "You've had a rough time too, haven't you?"

The question hangs in the air. Blood pounds

in my brain. *Yes*, I want to scream. *I've had a rough time too.* Am I more like Libby than I'd realized?

"So your birth mother died?"

"When I was five." I see the sadness in her face as she glances down at Maddie. Does she ever wonder what will happen to her own children if she dies? "Once you've filed charges—"

"I'm *not* pressing charges," she spits out, but I can tell she's near tears. "Besides, the kids miss their home. Right, Maddie? You want to go home and play with your own toys, right?"

Maddie looks up from the dollhouse. "No!"

I try to reason with her. "Honestly, Libby, we see this all the time. Once you go back, he'll be nice for a while but eventually start drinking or drugging or whatever his vice of choice is and take his frustrations out on you. Can't you see what you're doing?"

Oops. I've just broken Rule Number 1 of *philoxenia*: *No questions concerning their lifestyle are permitted.*

"You don't know Jax." Her voice has an edge to it. "You think I'm like all the rest, but I'm not." She dumps the folded onesies into the bag and stuffs a pink sweater on top. "I'm *not*."

The silence between us throbs like a toothache. I finally manage a weak suggestion.

"Maybe you could stay with your folks for a while."

"Yeah, right. My mom lives with a guy half her age in a one-bedroom flat on the West Coast. If I tell her what happened, she'll start bawling and blaming herself. She always said, 'I don't want you to go through what I did.' She dumped my dad years ago."

My throat tightens as all the feelings I have for Tee-tee overwhelm me. She doesn't beat us. She hasn't left us to fend for ourselves.

"Can't you dump Jax? Don't you hate him now?"

"No." Libby looks at me in amazement. "No, I don't hate him at all. I love him. You don't understand. Love doesn't go away overnight."

"But your dad—"

"Jax isn't like that. He loves us more than anything. He apologized and promised he'll never do it again."

Panic rises in my chest. "You called him?"

Libby nods, sniffling. "He needs us."

"Did you tell him where you are?"

Libby avoids my gaze. "No. Not really."

"Not really?"

"Not any street name or numbers."

Great. All he has to do is track the number she's called from and do a Google search for our

address.

If Tee-tee thinks she has deer problems, she'll have a cow when she hears this one.

"Damn deer," Tee-tee mutters, holding up her mangled bird feeder. "It's time to get serious. That buck seems to have adopted us. He's bringing the whole herd here."

I palm-slap my forehead. "Jeez, I've been adopted *twice*."

Tee-tee's in no mood for a joke. "Freaking deer. Oh, my poor apple trees." She fingers the tips of branches, twiggy ends twisted and shredded, stripped of new bark. "I've got to find something to keep those deer off our property. I can't fence the whole orchard."

"Why don't we plant stuff the deer don't like? Then they can still visit, but they won't eat."

"That's just the problem. In winter, when large herds are starving, they'll eat anything their mouths can reach."

"Libby's starving too. But I don't know what she needs."

Tee-tee snorts. "A swift kick in the knickers. A backbone. A smidgen of self-confidence would definitely help."

"She says Jax didn't mean to hit her."

"And we've all heard that sob story before."

Tee-tee mimics in a high, cloyingly sweet voice, "He really *loovves* us. He'll *neevvver* do it again. Load of crap."

"Why do women go back? Why doesn't Libby dump him? I don't get it."

Tee-tee leans her head back, letting the sunlight warm her face. "I've heard every excuse in the book, many more strange than the he-loves-me-won't-do-it-again ones. Some women feel they deserve to be beaten, that it's their own fault. Some have no skills and no way to support themselves. It's not easy to dump someone you have kids with and own joint property with. You've got to get a lawyer involved."

"But people get divorced every day. It can't be that hard."

"You're right, but that's if the divorce is between two people who can work out their settlement in a civilized manner, not with a spouse who settles things with his fists. Besides, some women fear for their furniture."

"Their furniture? What's with that?"

Tee-tee chuckles and shakes her head. "Can you believe it? They care more about their lumpy old sofas and grandma's buffet being trashed than they do about their own lives."

"Can't we force Libby to stay? Maddie doesn't

want to leave."

Tee-tee glances up at the house. Libby is standing at the bedroom window, in plain sight.

"She doesn't want to be here. And it's too dangerous for us to keep her here, especially since you say she's called him. Damn those cell phones. At least we had some control over phone rights before those blasted things were invented. She might not have given us away, but battered women in love tell all kinds of stories."

"We need a security system. We talk about it but never get one installed."

"I know, I know. I've been remiss."

"So what will you do?"

"I'm driving her to the police station, and they'll take it from there. Maybe they can talk some sense into her, get her to sign another Order of Protection. Just in case her husband's up to his old ways, lurking around the house."

*Or lurking around our house.* I shudder.

I stand by the garage door as Tee-tee backs out the Jeep. The driver's side window slides down. I wriggle my fingers at Maddie in the backseat, grunting and struggling against her seatbelt. Ethan grins and bats at an orange googly-eyed chicken dangling from his carseat. Libby stares

out the passenger side window, silent.

"Take care, Libby." She sniffs but doesn't acknowledge me. She lifts a tissue and dabs at her nose. I wonder what's running through her head and what's going to become of her. And if she'll be safe.

So much for Rule Number 3 of *philoxenia*: *When the time comes we send the guest safely on her way, making sure she reaches her destination and comes to no harm.*

"You've got the dryer sheets and the grater?" Tee-tee asks me.

I hold up a small laundry box and a cheese grater.

Tee-tee gives me a thumbs-up.

I have been ordered to drive off the deer, using eco-friendly repellents. The logic eludes me. Here at Philoxenia House, we welcome strangers. We feed them. We show them compassion. So what's wrong with welcoming a herd of hungry, hunted deer? Strangers are strangers, human or wild.

"I'll be back about four-ish," Tee-tee says, slowly rolling down the drive. "I've told Nikky to get his butt out here and help you."

As the Jeep motors off, a detached voice repeats in my head: *She'll be back she'll be back she'll be back.* They all do, if not in a few days or

weeks, then before the year is out. Unless they end up dead.

But the orchard awaits. It's a small one, as orchards go, dwarf varieties planted after I arrived here: Cortland, Winesap, Northern Spy, Macintosh. Tee-tee prunes them like an executioner in the spring, lopping off limbs with big shears, so they'll bear early and heavily. And because they're dwarf, they don't grow much taller than ten feet—a perfect height for deer. I've seen deer rear lightly on their hind legs and nibble, their black mouths stripping branches of sweet leaves and crunchy red globes.

It's not only the deer though. Every critter for miles loves our trees. Raccoons. Jays. Chipmunks. Last summer Tee-tee saw a squirrel scampering across the lawn with an apple in its mouth. She hurled her clog at it and missed, but hit the birdbath instead, knocking a chip off the rim. I'm always telling her to ease up and stop fighting a losing battle because, after all, we live in the *country* where we're outnumbered, not some sterile concrete city condo. But she gripes about how there are no natural predators anymore and maybe we should set catch-and-release traps and transport the offending critters to the state park where they can eat all the garbage left by

tourists. Or, on a day when she's particularly peeved, we can grind them into stew meat.

Something has nibbled the bark around the base of a couple trees. A rabbit perhaps. Tee-tee will not be happy. This means tree wrap, another expense. It would be cheaper to buy apples at the store, all polished and blemish-free, but I know Tee-tee will go all organic on me.

Nikky shuffles out into the cold, wearing sneaks and a short-sleeved T-shirt.

"Five minutes before *Fear Freaks* are on," he tells me. "What do you want me to do?"

"I've got news for you, Nik. It'll take longer than five minutes, so you'd better record it."

I know this isn't what he wants to hear. He expects me to cave and say, *That's okay, Nikky, I really don't need your help. Go back inside and watch TV. Anything for my sweet baby brother.* Won't happen. As long as I'm tapped to do Tee-tee's dirty work, he's going to be my A-Number One assistant.

"Oh . . . OK," he mutters. "Be back in a sec."

Twenty minutes later he's peering over my shoulder as I'm threading twisty-ties through the scented dryer tissues. He picks up the box and reads from it. "Repels hair and lint." He nudges me with his foot. "Deer have lint?"

"We tie the dryer sheets to the tree branches." I demonstrate by looping the twisty wire around the end of a branch. The attached tissue flutters in the breeze. "The scent repels the deer."

"So what's with the cheese grater? Serving the deer spaghetti while you rid them of static cling?"

Nikky can be annoyingly comic, and, if I weren't so ticked off about this chore, I'd probably egg him on. "To grate soap around the trunks. Same objective."

He reads off the box again. "*Sunshine Fresh.* At least we'll have the freshest-smelling trees in the neighborhood."

"It's an environmentally conscious form of pest control," I say solemnly, repeating Tee-tee's explanation to me. "It doesn't hurt them, just spooks them. It smells like humans."

Nikky holds a dryer sheet to his nose and sniffs it. "You and Mom both smell fresh as daisies. The deer don't seem to be afraid of you. It ain't gonna work, sis."

He has a point. The work is pointless.

"But Tee-tee will notice," I tell him, "and she won't be happy with that answer."

I rig up another twisty-tissue and loop it over a branch on the opposite side of the tree. Nikky

stands motionless, staring over my shoulder.

"Well, are you going to help or what?"

"We've got company, Darya."

I glance at the driveway. No one. I pivot to face behind me.

A semicircle of pale brownish-gray bodies surrounds us. They're quiet and rigid as statues. Black-tipped ears, a white patch under each throat.

"See," Nikky says, "I told you that stuff wouldn't work."

"Shh." I slash out my hand to hush him. "Quiet." He's right. They don't seem spooked at all.

Nikky's voice drops to a whisper. "Do you want me to get the pot?"

Their eyes are friendly, inquisitive. I know they can't understand me, not like dogs or cats seem to, but I try anyway. "What do you want?" I ask them, speaking in a soft, high voice as if to Maddie.

Nikky shifts a foot. "Don't *move*," I murmur with as much force as I dare. "They'll bolt."

One doe, braver than the others, steps from the thicket. She stares in my direction, ears swiveled forward, black nose sniffing the air with little dips and bobs. Sensing no danger she drops

her head and forages for the sparse greenery poking up where snow has melted off.

The others follow her lead, dropping their heads and nibbling.

"Hey, they like the chow here." Nikky reaches out to an apple tree and strips the dried brown leaves off an extended branch. "Here ya go," he says, tossing out a handful of leaves. A gust of wind whips them back at his face.

"Some host you are." I know exactly what they need, and I know where to get it. "Stay here, Nik. I'll be right back."

I keep up a friendly chatter, all the while sidling toward the door at the back of the garage. I step inside, then crouch and stuff my pockets from a wood-slatted crate. I fill the inside of my zipped-up parka, and my waist puffs out like a pregnancy. A silly thought enters my head: *Why yes, I'm due any time now with my first apple.* Maybe it'll make Libby laugh when I see her again.

I casually saunter back to Nikky's side, keeping a little sing-song monologue going. The deer skitter back, their ears cocked forward, tails switching. Finally the lead doe steps forward, nostrils quivering.

"Are you hungry?" I ask her. "Here's a treat

for you." I pitch the apple gently in her direction. She lifts her nose and shivers, whether from the scent of the apple or dryer sheets or me, I can't tell.

She steps toward me as if to snatch up the apple, but at the last minute whirls and retreats. She watches me over her shoulder. We stand regarding each other.

"Step back, slowly," I whisper to Nikky.

We take a few paces back. Finally she trots forward and stretches her neck out. She sniffs the apple, rolls it around with her nose, and licks it. The others watch as she opens her black lips and sinks her large teeth into the apple.

A car crunches up the icy drive. Tee-tee's home.

The doe's ears perk up, and she crouches, ready to spring. She looks at me and bobs her head.

*She's thanking me.*

With a bound, she's off through the pines with the others close behind.

"Stupid deer," Nikky says. "No wonder Mom wants them gone."

"They're smart and beautiful," I reply.

"They're all over the place, everywhere. I don't know why you think they're so special—they all look alike to me."

He's wrong. "Deer are as different as snowflakes. No two are alike." *And they like me,* I nearly tell him.

*The doe stops chewing and swallows in a single gulp. Her large brown eyes pop open and stare intently back along the path she just traveled with her sisters. She snorts, clearing the awful smells from her nose. One was heavy with strong flowers. The other sent a shiver up her flank. It smelled of danger, of creatures with claws and fangs.*

*Through the brush, she catches sight of some moving thing, stepping heavily. She tenses for the leap to safety.*

*It is only the male. He gives a snort and cuts the earth with his front hoofs. The doe grunts a friendly greeting, welcoming a family member.*

*I saw her, the doe snuffles. The young animal. She was with another of her kind. She offered food.*

*The buck whistles with pleasure.*

Tee-tee holds up the nearly empty apple crate. "My Northern Spy apples. My *expensive* Northern Spys." She reaches out and turns my chin toward her. "Where'd they go?"

Nikky and his big mouth.

"Darya? The truth, please."

"We had company." Somewhat the truth.

Tee-tee *tsks* and tosses the crate into a corner of the garage. It thunks against the trashcan.

I confess. "I fed them to the deer." No sense getting her more riled up by playing dumb.

"Honestly, sometimes I wonder why I ever—"

I know what's she's thinking: *adopted you.*

"Yes, they're destroying our shrubs and stripping the apple trees but—"

Tee-tee stops me with a shake. Heat emanates from her. Her flushed face is drenched in sweat. I'm afraid she might self-combust, burst into flames before my eyes with steam pouring out of her ears.

"Listen to me, Darya. Deer are beautiful creatures, but they're also flea-ridden pests. They destroy gardens and landscaping, fields of farm crops, and they carry Lyme disease ticks and the wasting disease. There are too many of them, and they end up getting hit by cars or attacked by dogs."

A cramp of anger seizes me. "But I had bugs and you kept me."

Tee-tee sways, then touches a hand to her forehead.

I reach out to steady her. "You need to see a doc—"

"What on earth do you mean, you had bugs?"

"When you came to Russia. When you bathed me. Remember? I had bugs. Ants in my pants. Parasites, just like the deer. We're no different." I don't add: *And you don't want them. Like you didn't want me.*

Tee-tee stands silent, eyes closed, breathing heavily. I can't tell if she's heard me. Or is remembering. Or is about to pass out.

She's scaring me. "Stay right here. I'm calling 911."

She grips my arm. "No." She squeezes out a lopsided smile. "It's a dizzy spell, that's all. One more old-lady symptom." She straightens up and throws her shoulders back. "See? All gone. Good as gold."

Tee-tee snaps a paper towel off the plastic dispenser on the garage wall and blots her forehead, under her chin, and the nape of her neck. "It's not the same. You're a person. They're wild animals. All animals have parasites. All

wild animals are hungry and must hunt for their food, not expect handouts from humans. Handouts make them lazy, unable to fend for themselves when the food supply is cut off. It's a fact of nature."

"But you feed birds. You make them rely on food you buy for them."

"Birds are small. Birds don't leap out in front of traffic. Birds don't use my orchard as an all-you-can-eat buffet."

Enough of this. I can't win. She has a comeback for everything, and I hate it. I wrench open the door leading to the kitchen and stomp inside.

Tee-tee calls after me. "Please don't shut me out. I'm your mother."

I hunch at the kitchen table, staring at the scratched wood, wishing I could take a sledgehammer to it. I squeeze my hands together until my knuckles turn white. Tee-tee comes in and stands behind me, then moves to the stove.

"I need a promise." Tee-tee fills a pot with water. "I want you to stop feeding the deer."

I can't do this. No freaking way.

"I'm trying to discourage the deer from coming here, and you're turning our place into a deer yard. Do you know what a deer yard is, Darya?"

She doesn't wait for a reply.

"It's a place where deer know they can always find food, a place where they congregate to eat, where they know no harm will come to them."

I knew she'd see my point. "Like Philoxenia House. A deer yard sounds good. We have lots of land. Why can't we have one? We'd shelter needy women *and* deer."

"Maybe someone else's yard, but not ours." Tee-tee wipes her hands on a dishtowel and turns to face me. "Promise you won't feed the deer again?" She touches my shoulder.

I fling her hand off with a twist. "I hate you."

I regret the words as soon as they leave my mouth.

Tee-tee gasps. "You'll do as I say, Darya." Her tone is curt and dictatorial, the phone voice she uses to reprimand welfare abusers.

"Fine," I say sharply. "I won't feed the deer." I wouldn't lie to my mother.

But Tee-tee isn't my real mother.

*The buck, three does, and two yearlings browse along the edge of the field. Apples. The buck sniffs the sweet fruity scent, but other odors intermingle. The young human touched these apples. But they also carry the vague scent of the large human who screeched at them.*

*A stray whiff of air reeks of human stench, of smoke, as when a fire blackened the woods one summer ago. His nose lifts as he strains to catch another scent. Dewdrops of moisture collect along the fringes of his nostrils, salty crystals that increase his ability to detect scent.*

*He drops his head and bites into the sweet flesh, crunching the frozen apple with his large white teeth. These are gifts from the young human, and he will not refuse them.*

# THE CHASE

**T**he doe stands wheezing and shivering at the edge of the lake. This is the end. She cannot go further.

She chops her forehooves into the shale beach and whips her head from side to side. Long scratches cut across her legs and flanks, lashed from the thorny wild raspberry canes she'd bounded through to escape. A wider gash slices across the fur at her neck. Droplets of blood spatter the smooth oval stones, tumbled and polished from water currents and erosion over the ages since glaciers receded.

She flings her head back and perks her ears toward the menacing howls and yelps. The dogs will soon be on her.

It was a mistake to cross the meadow near the young human's house. A sharp crack startled her, followed almost instantly by a razor of fire slicing across her neck, then the high-pitched whines of dogs begging to be released from their leashes.

She drops her muzzle to the wafer-thin crust of ice edging the beach. The water beyond this point is nearly black, reflecting the gunmetal gray clouds overhead. To her right is a beamed seawall topped with a wrought-iron railing. To her left, a dock and boat lift. A shiver seizes her and ripples across her flanks. She is trapped.

Here she will make her stand. She has no other choice.

Or does she?

She stares out over the wide expanse of water, to the tiny dots of seasonal cottages and covered boats in lifts on the opposite shore. A lone motorboat buzzes by, spraying plumes of water, as noisy as a hornet. When the world was warm and green, small humans plunged into the water and surfaced. They kicked and paddled toward shore, then splashed back in, over and over. They entered the water and lived. Could she do the same?

The dogs' sharp barks pierce the air, closing in.

She cannot wait a minute longer. She plunges her front hoofs through the icy crust. Wavelets lap over her legs as her hoofs slide on the loose gravel. The dogs are almost on her. She lifts her nose and catches their feral scent.

A dog crashes through the brush and rushes her. Three others follow. Snarling, they bound into the water and snap at her hindquarters. With a high-pitched shriek she kicks backward and makes contact. A yelp, and a thud to the ground.

The doe takes three long strides into the lake, up to her white underbelly. Danger lies ahead as well as behind. The cold black water might suck her down into her grave. But the far side of the lake holds the possibility of safety. Two more step forward. Icy waves wash over her back. Her hoofs scrumble at the gravel below as the tips barely touch, lifting and lightly bouncing like a ballerina en pointe. Weeds twine around her legs, and she kicks to break free. Open water offers no foothold, no gravel, no weeds. She stretches forward and dogpaddles, keeping her eyes on the far shore. With her head well above water, she swims briskly. Her powerful leg muscles propel her forward. Instinct keeps her buoyant, even though she has never tread water.

*The dogs bay and howl as they splash into the water after her. One paddles out several feet, cries* yip-yip-yip *at the cold, then turns and clambers back up the beach. They leap up on their hind legs, barking and whining as the doe moves across the lake. The hunt is over.*

*The doe noses forward with strong, steady strokes. Lips raised, she inhales in great gasps and strains toward the opposite shore. Her fear lessens with the dogs far behind. The buzzing drone of the motorboat drowns out their yelps.*

*She nears a craft bobbing at an orange buoy, silent like the ones tied with ropes to wooden docks on the other shore. She swims closer to cut* straight toward an empty swath of shoreline. The tips of her hoofs touch stones, and with a mighty lunge she pitches forward and struggles up the beach. Solid ground at last.

She springs into the dense thicket, then pauses and flings up her graceful neck. Her large bat-like ears shift in the direction of engine sounds. But the sounds move away, not toward her. She paws the ground, then snorts twice to clear her nostrils of water. She is safe.

Head high, she leaps through the woods in search of . . . who? She trots to a stop, fearful again. She has left her herd on the far shore. She is alone, an orphan, a stranger on this side of the lake. She lifts her nose and probes the air for others of her kind. But her nostrils clog with the harsh, sickening stench of exhaust and gasoline.

# Driving Lessons

Tee-tee rummages in her purse and pulls out her key ring. She tosses it to me in a casual underhand motion, as if it's something we do every day of the week. "Get your permit," she tells me. "I need a ride to Home Fix-It."

It takes a moment for the words to sink in. The furnace kicks on. The refrigerator's icemaker dumps cubes. I barely choke out my reply. "You're letting me drive?"

Tee-tee glares at me. "Am I mistaken, or aren't you the girl who's been hounding me to let her practice driving?"

"Yes!" I'm as happy as a puppy that sees its leash and hears the word *out*.

I'm off my chair and up the stairs before

she changes her mind. My learner's permit is tacked to my bulletin board, still residing in its official blue-lettered New York State envelope where it's been since Day One, awaiting this momentous occasion. I slip it out and press it to my lips, mostly to keep myself from throwing up with joy.

When I get back to the kitchen, Tee-tee is

shooing Nikky out the door. "Tell Jake's mom I owe her one. We'll be back in an hour." She's holding a metal tape measure and a slip of paper with pencil markings, dimensions for our replacement door.

As Nikky tromps through the snow to the neighbor's house, Tee-tee and I head to the garage. I circle the hood to the driver's side, running my hand along the Jeep's shiny black surface. My whole life is about to change. The key in my hand gives me a heightened sense of importance, as if I'd scratched off little squares on a lottery card to find I'd won the MegaMillion Jackpot.

But I'm jittery too, on edge, and a little unsure of myself. I would have preferred some advance warning, like *Darya, how would you like to practice driving tomorrow afternoon?* instead of having it sprung on me. No matter. I'm not about to back down now because who knows when Tee-tee might offer again.

The garage door grinds and creaks upward. I grip the steering wheel with one hand and lift myself onto the driver's seat. I love this Jeep, so high off the ground. I'm like royalty ensconced on my automotive throne. I insert the key in the ignition like I've seen Tee-tee do a million times. A quick twist forward. The engine catches and

purrs.

"Buckle up!" Tee-tee barks from the passenger seat, appointing herself the seatbelt police.

"Okay, okay." I reach behind my head for the webbed belt strap. *Snap.* "Got it." I point to her unbelted waist. "You next."

She digs in her purse and fishes out a tissue. She lifts her glasses, dabs at her eyes, and blots her brow. "Air. I need air." She punches the fan button, and frigid air blasts from the vents.

She's nervous—the sweat is a dead giveaway.

"Rule number one." She points to my feet. "Right pedal is the gas. Left pedal is the brake. Don't get them mixed up. And use your right foot only."

I roll my eyes and flop forward like a chastised rag doll. "Right, gas. Left, brake," I repeat through gritted teeth. "One foot. Got it."

"Don't take that tone with me, young lady. You'd be surprised at the number of accidents that happen because drivers got their pedals confused."

"No mixing of pedals here." I draw an X on my coat. "Cross my heart and hope not to die."

I catch a glimpse of myself in the rearview mirror. I have a smug smile on my face, like a kid who's about to open a birthday present but

already knows what's inside. I too know what I'm getting today: Freedom. I move the shift lever to *R*.

"Reverse! Reverse!" Tee-tee is clutching the dashboard now. "Easy on the gas. Slow and steady, Darya. Slow and steady."

I clamp my mouth shut. This is not going to be the pleasant driving experience I'd imagined. We're not even out of the garage yet, and my jaw is tensed tight as a spring. The fifteen-mile drive to Home Fix-It stretches out before me, looking a lot like Dante's highway to hell. I step on the gas, and the Jeep rolls backward faster than I'd expected.

"Slow, damn it!" Tee-tee's hand whips out and grips the steering wheel.

I stomp on the brake with both feet. My seatbelt cinches against my chest in the jerky pitch forward. Too bad, because at this moment I would rather die, with my embarrassed face smeared like a bug on the windshield. I'm a failure. I silently vow never to take Driver's Ed because the *F* will make me a laughingstock at school.

I ease my feet off the brake, and the Jeep continues its backward roll.

"Brake!"

I stomp. Both feet. The seatbelt is a boa constrictor, crushing my chest in its snaky embrace. I pray it will strangle me.

Tee-tee exhales. "Put it in park."

I engage the gear, snap off the ignition, and drop the key ring in Tee-tee's lap. "I quit. You drive."

"Nonsense." She launches into a soft-voiced lecture about how everyone makes mistakes the first time out, and how lucky I am to learn on an automatic because her first lesson was on a manual, a stick shift, that she bucked all over the parking lot, riding the clutch and grinding gears until they smoked. "My father lost his remaining hair because of that lesson. Three pedals for two feet. Can you imagine?"

This admission only makes me feel more of a klutz. Next she'll be reminding me how she typed all of her school reports, error-free with triplicate carbon copies, on a manual typewriter.

She holds out the key ring. "Let's try it again."

The driveway is clear, lined with clumps of ice-crusted snow. I stop where our drive meets the main road and check both ways before I back out.

Tee-tee's head cranes from side to side, back

to front. "All clear," she says in a rush of breath. She pats my arm. "You're doing fine, honey-bunny."

I give her a tight smile. "Thanks for the help."

I put the Jeep in drive and ease down on the gas. The road has been plowed and sanded, and the blacktop gleams under bursts of sunlight emerging now and then from the clouds. I flick on the directional signal for my turn. Taking a right onto Walnut is easy until a Lexus blows by me, passing on the left. I clutch the wheel, my knuckles almost popping through my skin.

"Student driver here!" Tee-tee yells. She shakes a fist at the receding car. "Slow the heck down, you jerk." She turns to me. "Did you see that, Darya? Did you see how dangerous other drivers can be?" She darts a look at her side-view mirror and mutters. "Maniac. We're going to be killed by some road hog. Probably on his cell. Texting."

I reach for the radio knob, but she slaps my hand away.

"Eyes on the road," she orders. "It's important to keep your eyes on the road and keep pace with traffic."

I'm under the speed limit, so I give it some gas.

"Slow down." She braces herself with one hand on the dashboard. "Don't tailgate the car ahead of you."

I clench my jaw and ease up on the gas. I drive in silence, sneaking a peek at her profile every so often, stiff-lipped and staring straight ahead. I am trying to do everything perfectly, exactly by the state driver's manual, which I have memorized down to the Highway Signs and Their Meanings. I want to ask her why she's so uptight about my driving, why she can't relax and offer some friendly instruction like *You might want to ease into the left lane* or *How about going a smidgen faster*. But no, I get drill sergeant commands instead.

By the time we get to the highway entrance ramp, Tee-tee comes back to life. "Turn on your headlights," she says. "That knob on the left." She exhales in a whoosh and smiles at me. "You're doing great, Darya." Tears trail down her cheeks.

Tee-tee's waterworks are totally unexpected. I swerve over the yellow line. "Tee-tee, what's wrong?"

She honks into a tissue. "I'm so proud of you, and you're so grown up now. I remember when you fell off your bike after I removed the training wheels." She stares off into space and sighs. "It

all went so fast, those years when you were little and needed my protection. And now you're driving, and . . ." She fidgets with the tissue in her lap.

"And what, Tee-tee?" Tiny granules of snow hit the windshield in a sudden burst, but clear just as quickly. The Jeep's back end swerves, then catches on dry pavement. I stifle an urge to stomp on the brake. I long to take in Tee-tee's face, but I have to focus on the slick highway.

"And you'll be going away to college soon and leaving me."

"But that's years away, Tee-tee!"

"Sweetie, when you're my age, years fly by like days."

This seems impossible to me. So far, high school has been interminable.

"But it's good that you're driving," Tee-tee continues, "because you'll be able to shop for me and cart your brother around."

A warmth rushes through me at the thought of having these adult driving responsibilities. "I'd love to. Anytime."

"And I wanted to see that you had your driver's license before I die."

I clutch the steering wheel in a death grip. My right foot hovers over the brake. Or is it my left foot? "Die? You're *dying*?"

"Well, not right at this instant," she says. "But you know I'm going through menopause now, don't you?"

"Yes, but that's not dying, right? You're only *changing*."

Tee-tee sighs. "Changing, yes. Losing my estrogen and turning into a wise old crone. No longer a young, attractive chick like yourself."

Her chuckle lightens the mood, but a black emptiness worms its way into me. I can't bear the thought of losing another mother—even a substitute one.

*The doe stops near a grove of birches where a granite ledge towers above her like a great wave, speckled pink, black, and white in the fading light. The dogs are far behind, across the large water. Their cries are faint, barely audible. Although the exertion warmed her, the sun is low in the sky, covered by clouds, and she shivers. Swimming across the lake took all her energy and depleted her body's reserves. She must find food. She must rejoin her herd.*

*She crouches, then springs up the slope, her hoofs slipping on the rocky debris. A landslide of stones tumbles behind her. When she reaches the crest of the ledge, she looks down, one forehoof up. Her hind legs quake from fear and weakness, and she inhales a dozen short breaths. In the valley formed by two rolling ridgelines, a ribbon of highway stretches in the distance with dots of moving lights.*

*She slowly descends and silently moves through the woods. She cannot rest. If she does, her body may never move again. A lethargy she has never felt before falls over her like a black shroud. She lifts her head and tests the scents. The air currents carry no scent of the wild, of her kind. Only the acrid stink of exhaust from the moving lights. But the lights mean humans, and, perhaps, food.*

"So what do you think will happen to Libby?" I glance over at Tee-tee who by now seems calm, although her eyes are still glued to the road.

She sniffs before answering. "If past

114

experience is any indicator, she'll be back with her husband, going through the same rigmarole."

"Will she come back to our house, or will they take her to another shelter?" I don't know why I care so much about Libby. We've had lots of guests stay with us over the years. But something about Libby is different. She has potential. She can *be* something better. Something other than a punching bag.

"Depends. I told Social Services to put me on the Last Call list."

I flick my directional, check my mirrors, and move into the left lane. I step lightly on the gas and ease past the slower moving traffic on the right. Tee-tee doesn't carp at me but seems aware that I can multitask now: talk *and* drive.

"What's that mean, Last Call?"

"Meaning I'm the backup house if the other shelters are full. I think it's about time I phase out of this domestic violence business, Darya. I'm getting too old for it, and too harsh."

"But you're not, Tee-tee. Harsh, I mean. You're a creampuff. And you're so kind to our guests and help them put their lives back together."

"It may seem that way on the outside, but inside I'm seething with frustration. I want to rage at them and read them the riot act. After all

these years, I've finally realized that no matter what I do for these women, the majority go back into the same situations they came out of. It's a never-ending battle." She pounds on her thigh. "It's such a waste of my time." Then softer: "I'm feeling like a failure, Darya. I set out wanting to make the world a better place, but all I've done is put you and Nikky in danger."

I can't believe what I'm hearing. "But I love what you do, Tee-tee. I love having guests. I've never felt that we were in danger when you were in charge."

"I'm growing less in charge every year, less able to handle these cases." She shifts in her seat and throws her shoulders back. "So that's why I'm on the Last Call list. Philoxenia House is on its way to extinction, like an old dinosaur."

*She begins the long descent down the hillside that takes her to a metal barrier bordering the edge of a roadway. Several times she slipped and fell onto her side. Her flanks are bruised and caked with mud. Her breath comes in deep gasps. Her tongue protrudes from the side of her*

*mouth.*

*She must find water and food. With a burst of strength, she leaps over the barrier.*

*She is struck.*

*The impact hurtles her against the metal barrier. The car veers onto the shoulder, its tires spitting loose gravel, then swerves back onto the asphalt. A lick of flame sears her left shoulder. She staggers to her feet and weaves in weakness, swaying as if she will topple.*

*Crazed with pain she crashes blindly down the road toward a concrete abutment. Her body heaves with each breath, and she shoots forward with every ounce of her strength. She flings her head back to clear her eyesight, but blood gushes from the wound on her head. If she can cross the concrete barrier, she'll be free. Free to climb the hills that tower above, growing shadowy in the twilight. She must jump. Her stride draws up, and she kicks out to lunge toward the far hills. As she sails forward, her knees buckle under her and scrape the concrete.*

*For a moment she is airborne, flying like the sparrows in her woods, like the squirrels that leap from branch to branch.*

*Then she falls. She falls. She falls.*

*When she hits the asphalt highway, her chest implodes with a thud.*

"Take the next exit," Tee-tee tells me, "right after this overpass."

I stay in the right lane, cruising comfortably at 65 until a wave of brake lights flash red on the back ends of the cars ahead of me. The rig that blew by me in the passing lane starts a slow-motion jackknife on the slick road.

*She rises to her knees and strains to lift herself. She stumbles and collapses onto her forelegs. Blood trickles from her black nostrils. Inside her belly, something feels loose and watery, as though all the ligaments and organs that hold her together have liquefied. She weeps oily tears as moving lights speed toward her, blinding her. A cold metal grille hammers her head-on. Her flanks explode in pain.*

"Slow down," Tee-tee barks, peering forward in concentration.

I slam on the brakes, and Tee-tee screams as we fishtail crazily across the wet pavement. The bottom of my stomach drops out as if our flight has hit an air pocket. We skid across the shoulder and swerve to an abrupt sideways stop. The lurch makes my gut somersault. An instant later the car behind us hits the ditch to our right and topples onto its side. Tires squeal, quickly followed by the *screeeak* of crushing metal. Cars behind us collide in a chain reaction.

I squirm in panic. "Tee-tee?" She's slumped against the door. "Tee-tee, wake up."

She twitches and mumbles something I can't make out. Her eyes blink, and she turns to look at me. Her face glows a ghastly green from the dashboard lights. She's blank with shock.

I grab a handful of her wool coat and give her a shake. "Tee-tee!"

With a gasp, she snaps to. "What? What happened?" She twists in her seat and surveys the mess over her shoulder. Her mouth gapes in disbelief. She turns and presses a warm hand to my face and glides it down my arm. "Are you okay? Are you hurt, baby?"

"Fine. I'm fine." I click the release on my

seatbelt and struggle out of the strap. "Let's get out and check the damage." I fumble for the door handle.

Tee-tee grips my arm. "No. We have to stay here until the police come."

"That could be a while. And besides, someone might be hurt."

Tee-tee stares at me for a split second until her Type-E personality kicks in. "You're right. Let's go."

We're out of the Jeep and hustling down the shoulder of the highway, eerily lit by car headlights. Icy wind whips open my coat and pelts my face with tiny granules of stinging sleet. Sirens wail in the distance, along with the low *onk-onk* of a fire truck, faint at first, then louder as they approach the scene. We bow our heads into the wind and struggle forward to the head of the line of cars just short of the overpass. A small group of dazed onlookers circles a large brown mass splayed in the middle of the highway. A dark red stain flows across the pavement.

Tee-tee shoves through the group and groans. She blocks me with her body, arms out, then quickly turns and grips my shoulders. "Go back to the Jeep, Darya." Her voice is husky, rimmed in pain. "You don't want to see this."

She's wrong. Whoever it is, I need to see. I

can deal with blood and pain. I see blood and pain every time we shelter a battered guest at Philoxenia House. Someone like Libby might be lying there, needing my help. I wrench away from Tee-tee and push past her.

The headlights of the lead car throw a blinding twin beam across the dark furred mass in the road. I suck in a breath. Cold air paralyzes my lungs. I can't breathe.

The body splayed on the pavement is not human.

An open black eye gleams as an oily secretion trickles from it. Blood gushes from the doe's mouth. Her hind leg juts out at an awkward angle. I edge forward and drop to one knee, close enough to feel the heat radiating from her belly. A shiny loop of intestines is pinned beneath her. A wind gust carries the meaty, rank scent of bloody flesh and muck.

Tee-tee orders me not to touch the doe, but her words flit by me. I extend my fingers slowly, and stroke the fur on her foreleg. She quivers at my touch. I run my hand down her back to the ragged gash on her flanks. Her chest heaves unexpectedly. With a frightened gasp I pitch backward onto my butt.

Her eyelid flutters, and she rolls an eye to look at me. Her black eye bores into me. The edge

of her mouth lifts as if in greeting. The sirens and voices fade into nothingness as a buzzing fills my head. She wants to tell me something. I'm sure of it. I lean in and place my ear near her mouth, but the only sound is a strangled gurgle of breath clogged with fluid. Instead, words form in the depths of my head. A silent thought.

*Help me. Save me.*

"She's alive," I cry out. "We can save her." I move to a crouch, swivel on my heels, and plead with whoever will listen.

A balding man dabs a paper towel at his gashed forehead. A slender woman supports her neck at a stiff angle. A teen dry heaves at the side of the road.

"Somebody. Please help her."

Red lights strobe over blank stares. I can't expect them to help. They have their own troubles, their own wounds. Why should they care about a messy lump of roadkill? They've probably sped by hundreds of deer carcasses before, not giving them a second glance. And the drivers who escaped injury? They've no doubt already left the scene, eager to be heading home, thankful they were spared an insurance nightmare.

EMTs and fire fighters make their way down the line of vehicles, rapping on windows, freeing the remaining injured from their cars,

kneeling over unconscious bodies, lifting them onto stretchers and into ambulances. Tee-tee's back is hunched over a toddler bawling for her mommy. It's clear to me in this moment: Human lives rank first, animals second—or not at all.

Shiny black boots appear next to me, and a hand touches my shoulder. I look up at a navy parka bearing an NYS Police insignia looming over me. "She's pretty busted up," says a deep, official-sounding voice. "We'd better put her out of her misery."

I curl my head to my knees and squeeze my eyelids shut, burying my face in my arms, a tight ball of pain. I know he's right. I know it's the merciful thing to do, not to allow an animal to suffer.

But I can't get it out of my head that she wants to live.

*The doe's energy ebbs away; her light dies. Her body constricts in a spasm. Her legs kick out convulsively. Finally her muscles relax, her body goes limp.*

*But in the last instant, as she straddles the line between life and death, a joyful thought flits through her mind . . .*

*The small human who kneels at my side strokes me in a blessing way. Can it be? Is this the Dar-Ya spoken of by the herd? Is this our beloved ancestor reborn? How did she find me in my hour of death?*

*She must be of us because she is kind and unafraid. Her eyes weep for me. She cannot save me now. My time is over. But I so want to tell her how much we adore her.*

*Lean in again, Dar-Ya, and hear my words.*

The officer helps me up and gives me a gentle shake. "You okay, miss?"

I'm not, but I give him a quick nod. A frigid wind gusts across the highway, and I dig into my coat pocket for a tissue to staunch my runny nose before the snot freezes on my upper lip. It's too late for the tears iced on my eyelashes.

"I should probably call the DEC to handle this," he says, reaching to his hip, "but that might take a while, and she's in bad shape." He waves an arm at the shivering crowd. "Everyone back! Everyone stand back now!" He turns to me again. "You too, miss. Back you go." He gives me a gentle shove, and I stumble a few steps backward.

I will not hide my eyes. She deserves a witness to her death, someone who loves her. Me.

The officer lowers his revolver to the doe's head, but before he can pull the trigger, she heaves her last breath. I silently thank the Universe for allowing her to die on her own terms.

"Why did she leave the field?" I ask him as he backs away toward his squad car. "What makes them leap out into traffic when the field is safe?"

"She wasn't in the field." The officer points a finger upward. "Witnesses said she jumped from

the overpass."

*Jumped from the overpass.* The words slam into me like a jackknifing rig. I can see the evidence with my own eyes. But *why?*

For a long time, hours it seems, I stand with Tee-tee in the gathering dark and cold and watch over the rigid doe, until they cart her away in a town truck used for waste removal, her brown coat smeared with frozen blood.

# A good day to Die

**I**'m slung into the back of the truck with the deer carcass. I open my mouth to scream, but the sound is trapped inside my head: *I'm alive. Can't you see? I'm alive.* The driver billows a plastic tarp over the truck bed, blacking out the icy white pinpoints of stars. I claw furiously at the plastic, but it's slick as coffin satin, tightening to a rigid sheath as the driver lashes the corners down. I press my hips against the truck bed and thrust my feet up. The plastic crackles, bulges, and springs back. *Tee-tee!* I scream her name in my head. *Help me.*

The driver's door opens and slams shut. The engine catches, and we lurch forward. I reach out to stroke the doe's pelt, seeking her dying warmth.

The space is empty.

An oceanic roar fills my head, engulfs me. In the flick of an instant the truth paralyzes me. I am the sole carcass in this rumbling black crypt. I have taken her place. My coat is sticky with coagulating blood, my guts spill from my belly...

Above me, a bubble of light. I burst through it, gasping, jackknifed on the bed—*my* bed, not a truck bed of roadkill—my legs tangled in the twisted sheet. Claws dig into my nightshirt. Kitty leaps from my chest to the foot of the bed. She hisses, back arched. I want to soothe her, but my mouth is dry as sawdust, my tongue a thick slab of meat. All I can croak out is a raspy grunt, but it's a huge relief, proof that I'm really and truly alive.

I sweep my sweat-soaked hair into a knot at the back of my head and sink back into my pillow. Jittery spasms shoot through my calves. When I close my eyes, the jolt of my nightmare returns. I can't sleep. I doubt that I'll ever be able to sleep again.

So what can I do but lie here in bed listening to the familiar house sounds? The mantel clock bongs three times. The furnace kicks on. House timbers groan and pop. Something heavy pads up my belly, hunches on my chest, and digs its claws lightly into my nightshirt. Her purr sets up a rhythm I can breathe to, like Tee-tee does

in meditation: *In–two-three-hold. Out–two-three-hold.* I run my hands over kitty's back, then down my sides. I'm not bloody. My intestines are still tucked tightly inside. I'm alive, not dead.

A weight like an anvil presses down on my brain. My thoughts drift on a plane between reverie and sleep, eddying around a black hole. I give myself over to it and circle down, down, down again . . .

. . . and awaken on a path edged with raspberry canes and lush lacy ferns. Threads of heat lightning flash over the treetops. The air is still and hot. The sun burns orangey-red, low on the horizon, and I sense that it is evening, late June or early July, like the White Nights of my Russian childhood.

Oh, my bones ache! Each step down the path is a stab of pain. My bare foot snags on a thick black vine with curly tendrils, and I stagger and crash to the earth. My head thunks against an outcropping of rock. I've stirred up a cloud of mosquitoes that dives in to feast on my sweaty naked skin, sucking up blood with every jab. I slap at them, but it riles them even more, and they dig into my armpits and crawl into my ears and nose. Bloody welts cover my limbs. I give up. I can't muster the energy to fight anymore.

I would rest here forever, but the herd is waiting for me. I crawl now, dragging myself down the path to a grassy bank. Beyond the bank a pond shines like polished gold. I would like a swim. The thought of cool water on my itchy, swollen limbs energizes me. I hunker down on my haunches at the water's edge. The surface of the pond is glassy, disturbed only by the dip-dip of a dragonfly ruffling the surface. I tip my head over the edge to lap at the water. The reflection sends me sprawling backward.

*I* am not a girl.

I creep toward the pool again and inch my head over the water. An enormous rack of forked antlers appears above a doe's face, *my* face. In this world of dreamtime, I am something absurd, something freakish: a crossbreed of girl and beast with the torso of a human and the head of a deer.

How old I've become. My muzzle is grayed. In my stumble, one of the tines at the fork of my left antler has fractured and hangs by a shred of ruptured velvet. Blood streams down my face into my eyes and creeps into my nostrils. Deerflies cluster and bite, sucking my blood for their babies. Now I understand why my thoughts of bounding across the fields are only dim memories. Today I am barely able to stand. The weak sun's heat penetrates to my old bones. Vultures circle overhead, hungry as mosquitoes and deerflies, waiting to dine on my remains.

*Chooof!*

A sneeze interrupts my reverie. A buck, my beloved prince and consort, stands at the pond's edge watching me. A herd of does, yearlings, and fawns graze in the meadow behind. He snorts and shakes his massive rack, then sneezes again.

*Choof!* Summer grass pollen covers him like ash. For a moment he stands, waiting for my signal, his muzzle lifted.

I beckon him, and he trots to stand beside me.

*Yes, my Queen?*
*Help me, please?*

He sniffs me and licks my face with a long rough tongue, abrasive as sandpaper. He gently grasps the scruff of my neck in his large teeth and lifts me from the grass. My bones scream in pain, but I set my feet in motion and hobble toward a damp grassy patch beneath a tall oak twined with wild grapevines. I crumple beneath it in the cool shade. He nudges me to sit, and I settle myself on the gnarled roots, leaning against the tree for support. My legs are stretched out in front of me, and my antlered head is propped against the bark, tines rising like tree branches.

With every movement comes new pain. I drift in and out of consciousness. My time is near. This is a good day to die.

Jacqueline Horsfall

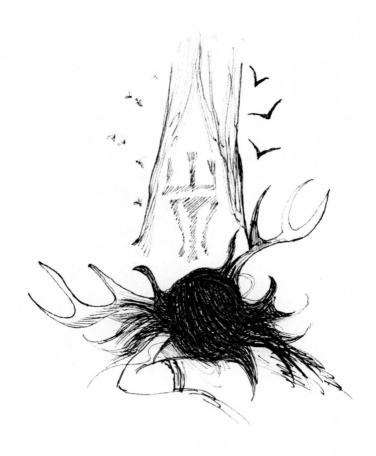

I open my eyes to the hum of a thousand bees harvesting nectar in the wild honeysuckle bushes. A spiraling tower of bees swirls upward. Their roaring buzz charges the air with a current so alive that it pulses in my veins. The bees convulse once, twice, then solidify into a distorted humanoid figure. A Lady of Bees. Her eyes drill into me with the cold warmth of glaciers melting into a summer sea.

*Don't be afraid, Daughter*, comes a soundless voice.

A single file of bees breaks away and streams toward me.

*Don't move, Daughter. Fear not.*

They buzz around my head and land on me. I clench all my muscles against the urge to slap at them. Their stingers probe my skin with tiny pricks. My skin twitches as they crawl over every inch of me, their sticky feet dabbing a gummy viscous gel. The cool ointment anesthetizes me, numbing my itchy welts.

*What is it?* I call to her. *What have you done to me?*

*You know this, Daughter, but you've forgotten.*

*Forgotten? What have I forgotten?*

*Royal jelly*, she replies. Her form spirals into

a cyclone as the worker bees rejoin her. *When the old queen is dying, a new queen must be born. Goodbye, Daughter. Die well.*

The sun explodes in a fiery burst that silhouettes her. In the ebon depths of her form writhe a mass of tangled, broken bodies—humans, animals, insects—singing a joyful lament for the sorrows of the world. The chanting vibrates something inside me, in a place strange and deep. I tremble in tune with their fear and longing. I am the Lady of Bees, and she is me. Her form twists upward into a thin column, then swiftly flattens as the bees return to the honeysuckle bushes.

My herd stands in a semicircle around me. My heart is near to bursting. My overwhelming love for them mingles with sadness. I must leave them.

Over the humming bees they chant:

*Enter, O Lady of the Forest, into our hearts and spirits*
   *All our lives long*
   *For we are You*
   *And You are us*
   *Your name we guard*
   *As a charm in our hearts*
   *Dar-Ya*

A doe steps forward, her kind brown eyes leaking oily tears. *Stay with us, Lady!*

I lift a hand toward her, palm up, and give my blessing. *Never fear. I will never let anyone hurt you. I will always protect you. I will return someday.*

An ash-black cloud passes over the sliver of remaining sun. A shiver rattles my cold bones. Thunder rumbles. The earth quakes beneath me as if vomiting up its dead. The herd steps closer and drops to their knees before me.

*Rah.* The whisper barely escapes my lips. *Rah.*

My prince bows his head toward me. *Yes, my Queen?* He rests his muzzle on the skin of my frail neck. One black marble eye stares down at me.

*Rah.* My last breath comes in a great exhalation as my soul escapes, my spirit lifts to the heavens. *Rah-Lee!*

Everything fleshly has been burned away. I am incandescent. My essence breaks free of my body like a kaleidoscope of white butterflies escaping an imprisoning net. The herd below—my family, my children—grieve over my corpse. I am dead. But I am alive!

I am *free*.

# The Legend of the

# One Who Will Save Us

As retold by
The Whitetail Deer of the Northeastern United States

Gather round, O Brothers and Sisters of the forest
And delve deep into your dreams of long ago
Of the Ancient One who is eternal and will come again
To protect us
To feed us
To save us

From the primeval forest she awoke, the Antlered One,
She of the horned goddesses, half human, half wild,
Lady of the Beasts
Who watched over us and protected us
From our clawed and fanged enemies
Who would maim and devour us
From the poison-tipped arrows and smoking metal sticks
That snuffed out our lives in a single instant
Or left us to die slow, lingering deaths

At the end of Her time, as she lay prostrate
on her bed of new-fallen leaves
The Ancient One promised, Her solemn vow:
"Never fear. I will come again, after many generations,
To protect you
To feed you
To save you.

And we await Her promise and watch for Her
Passing Her memory and words to our children
And our children's children
So they will not forget.

Now, she has come,
Born in the form of a human girl-child
Who awoke in our homeland, across the great water
Knowing our distress, she flew to us, and lives among us
She is born again, our Ancient One
She has fulfilled Her promise
She protects us
She feeds us
She will save us
And to show our joyful gratitude

We will protect Her.

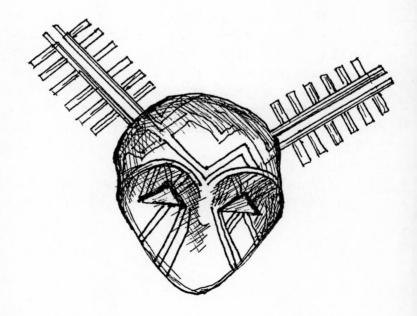

# HAMMER BOY

"Why the sad face, Darya?" Tee-tee asks as I stand at the counter and dump cereal into a bowl. "You're not still upset about yesterday, are you?"

"No," I lie. Something pricks at the edge of my mind, a fragment of a dream. A titmouse pecks at the kitchen window, and I catch my reflection in the dark glass, backlit by the ceiling light. Superimposed above my head, branching like forked antlers, is the skeleton of our Spy apple tree. A ghostly deer-girl stares back at me. The coffeemaker hisses a whisper of words. *We are You. You are us.*

"What's stuck in your hair?" Tee-tee's fingers tug something out of my tangles. "Cripe!" She flinches, then swats my shoulder.

I dance away, brushing frantically at my shoulders, slapping at my chest. "What? What is it?"

A curled black and yellow comma hits the floor. A comma with wings. And a stinger.

"Damn, they must be nesting behind the paneling again." Tee-tee scoops up the bee with a tissue and drops it in the trash. "They seem to revive as soon as the furnace ducts heat up."

A fragment of dream bobs to the surface. *Or as soon as their queen dies.* My hand shakes as I pour milk. It sloshes on the counter.

"Here, let me." Tee-tee sponges up the spill. "I know you're concerned about the deer," she says, wringing the sponge out in the sink, "but they'll survive just as they have for centuries. Sure, lots of them are hunted or hit by autos every season, but they're certainly not going extinct. Deer are smart, in their own way. They know how to survive among humans."

That's my Tee-tee, the eternal optimist. She could be clinging to the railing of the Titanic, and she'd still be raving about the beauty of icebergs.

I smack my hand flat on the counter. "How *smart* is a deer that belly flops off an overpass? That's asking for extinction. Why would an

animal kill itself on purpose?"

Tee-tee leans back against the sink and blows on her steaming coffee. "You're right, it's crazy strange. I can't say I've ever heard of such a thing before, but deer get spooked easily. This morning's early news reported another break-in like ours. A young buck busted through the glass door at Wayman's Jewelry & Gifts and tore the place up. The owner was asleep in her apartment above the store. She thought it was a burglary and called 911." She sips from the mug, grimaces, then stares intently into the black liquid as if reading omens. "If I didn't know better, I'd say something was . . . wrong. Very wrong."

"What do you mean, wrong? Wrong how?"

"Hard to say. I've heard of deer behaving strangely before, but this season they seem, well, *frantic*. Like they've been whipped into a frenzy." She tosses her head back and barks a laugh. "Almost like they're high on Mary Jane."

Tee-tee might be onto something. "You mean like an addict? You think someone's feeding them marijuana?"

"Or amphetamines." She holds a thumb-and-pinkie phone to her cheek and says in her official director voice, "Hello, Officer? We seem to have a herd of stoned deer on our property. Smoking weed. Yes, you heard me right. Potheads. Space

cadets."

"But jumping from an overpass? Into traffic? That's not how druggies act, is it?"

Tee-tee turns serious. "It depends on the drug. Back in the '60s, kids high on LSD thought they could fly out of sixth-floor windows." She shrugs. "Drugging deer isn't too likely. My guess is overly aggressive hunters, or maybe being chased by packs of stray dogs."

I spoon cereal into my mouth and chew. It gives me a moment to think. Tee-tee has talked around the problem but doesn't really answer the question. She feels it too—something is wrong—and we both know it's more than hunters or dogs. I swallow, then hit her with a bombshell. "She spoke to me."

"You mean that officer with the clipboard? Did she want our address?"

"The doe."

Tee-tee's hand jerks and coffee sloshes to the floor. "Now you know that's impossible."

Coffee seeps under Tee-tee's slippers, but neither of us makes a move. Here we stand in our nice warm house with its *Posted* yard and a garage filled with apples. A safe place the doe will never know. Never know because she's dead. "She asked me to save her."

Tee-tee clunks her mug down hard on the

counter. "I've had about enough of this nonsense. Deer cannot transmit thoughts. They do not speak to humans. They don't even *like* humans. We kill and *eat* them." She reaches over and snaps a paper towel off the roll, then presses it against her sweaty brow. Her chest is heaving, and I'm so hoping I haven't induced a heart attack. "And even if deer could communicate— which they *can't*—why would a crazy deer turn herself into roadkill just so she could ask a favor of you?"

I crunch another spoonful of cereal, so I won't have to answer. I knew she wouldn't understand. Why did I even bother telling her? I know exactly what she's thinking now: What on earth possessed me to adopt such a wacko space cadet?

"You've got a soft side for critters," Tee-tee says sweetly, giving me a quick squeeze to clear the charged air. "Maybe you'll be a vet."

I stiffen and lean away. I hurt inside, as if my heart has been pitched off an overpass and splatted on asphalt.

"You did a great job driving yesterday, sweetie. You handled a tough situation just like a pro. I'm really proud of you." She places a finger under my chin and tips my head up. "I'm lucky to have you and Nikky. You know that,

don't you?"

I nod, mouth full, and stare over her head. I know the real score. First Prize—Nikky. Consolation Prize—me.

As I mop up the floor with paper towels, Tee-tee stares out the window at the new bird feeder where a swarm of chickadees flutter and dart at seed. Yet she doesn't seem to see them. She looks sad, her face lined and pouchy. I should say something nice, but my tongue is paralyzed. I can't get the words out. Tee-tee sniffles, and her head droops. A tear hangs suspended on her fleshy cheek for a moment, then splashes into the sink.

We move around the kitchen in silence as we clear away the breakfast dishes and load the dishwasher.

"I think I'll work out at the Y this morning," she says finally. "I need the exercise." She pinches a roll at her waist and jiggles it. "I swear that after the holidays nothing but chicken broth will pass my lips for at least a week."

This comes as a total surprise. Tee-tee hasn't been to the Y in years, even though she has an annual guest pass courtesy of Social Services. I'm not sure what she expects me to say in response. *No, you're not fat? Yes, you need the exercise?* Instead I ask, "Do you want me to drive you?"

"No, no. But I'd appreciate it if you'd keep an eye on your brother while I'm gone." She opens the mudroom door and steps out. She rummages through the drawers under the bench. "Now where is it? Where's my gym bag?"

"You can use mine," I call out. I don't want to tell her I've trashed her bag by hauling apples in it.

As the Jeep backs out of the drive, I sit at the computer and compose an e-mail for our local newspaper's Op/Ed page:

Dear Editor:

I'm writing in protest of the D. E. E. R. (Deer Early Extermination Resolution) passed by the town board. Am I the only person in this community who cares if deer live or die? Shouldn't deer have the right to live in peace, as gentle creatures of our planet?

I've heard all the gripes: Deer are pests. Deer are nuisance animals. Deer carry disease. Deer cause auto accidents. Deer eat crops and landscaping.

So let's kill them.

Is that the only answer? Do we have the right to kill creatures just because we don't like their natural habits?

Here's what I believe: Hunting causes more

harm than good. Hunted, scared deer dart across the roads, causing more auto accidents. Hunters trespass on posted properties, sometimes shooting too close to houses and injuring people inside. Hunting spooks deer into doing weird stuff like busting through glass doors, wandering through gift shops, leaping from overpasses, and even attacking humans.

We've stolen their land, their habitats. We've built our houses and roads on their grazing land. We've tempted them with an all-you-can-eat buffet of delicious landscaping. Now we want them obliterated.

I don't know about the rest of you, but I'm sick of this way of thinking. I protest D. E. E. R.

Sincerely,
Darya Malakovsky Tomasio
Junior, Twin Lakes High School

I click SEND.

I stare at the Weather Channel, hypnotized by my favorite hottie, a forecaster bundled up in a puffy parka, the faux fur hood framing his gorgeous face. He waves a gloved hand and shoots the camera an *ain't-this-great?* grin as he's buffeted by wind gusts. The noon forecast

predicts an early Arctic cold front originating in Siberia, pushing south over Canada and into upstate New York. *Great.* I mentally prepare myself for a snow day tomorrow. I can't wait to burrow under my warm covers when Tee-tee's alarm goes off.

Nikky plods downstairs in his sweats. He yawns and scratches his crotch. "Mom!" he yells, his voice gravelly with sleep. "Can you drive me to Dollar Shopper?" He shuffles over and stands between me and the tube. "Where's Mom?"

"Tee-tee's at the Y." I motion him away from the TV. Mr. Hottie Forecaster is circling his hunky arm in the pattern of a Nor'easter.

"For a meeting? When's she coming back?"

"Not for a meeting. To work out."

Nikky gives me a bug-eyed stare. "Mom's working out? You mean like exercising? Pumping iron?" The thought seems to astound him.

"Probably just the treadmill. She's feeling fat."

"She is *not* fat."

I hold up a hand. "Whoa. She said it, not me."

Nikky crosses his arms, clearly outraged. "That's stupid. She's not fat. She's . . . curvy. She's the most perfect, curvy Mom in the whole world."

I agree with him, to keep the peace. "Yep, Tee-tee's the best."

"*Mom's* the best," Nikky says with finality.

It's cute the way he sticks up for Tee-tee, like a loyal knight defending his queen. I've read that boys and their mothers—even their adoptive mothers—are tight. They have some special bond that's missing in mother-daughter relationships. One more strike against me.

"So can you take me, Darya? To Dollar Shopper? I need a folder with pockets for school."

This is a ruse. He'll be in the DVD aisle before I can unzip my coat. I slump back on the couch. "No driver's license, remember? And anyway, Tee-tee's got the Jeep."

"Oh yeah, right." He thinks for a moment. "Well, how about we hike it and cut across Sandore's field?"

"We can't. It's hunting season. It's too dangerous to be out in the fields now. Wait till Tee-tee gets home, and she'll drive you."

"Sandore always posts his land." Nikky waves me off. "No hunters allowed. Besides, his property borders the Dollar Shopper parking lot. No one would dare shoot that close to a shopping center full of people."

"But Tee-tee said—"

"Oh, c'mon, Darya." He drops onto the cushion and snuggles against me like when he was a toddler. "Pleeeze? I'll wear my orange vest like the hunters do. You can wear that ugly pink parka Aunt Barbara gave you last Christmas. No hunters will mistake *us* for deer." He tugs on my arm. "Pretty please, with cherries on top?"

My better judgment tells me Tee-tee will be furious, but then how could things be any worse between us? It simply isn't in me to blame it all on Nikky. I'll tell her I was bored and needed a shopping fix and talked Nikky into accompanying me because, yes indeedy, the school requires that every student possess a folder with pockets. Besides, I can stand a little exercise myself, as long as it doesn't involve any diving deer.

"Okay, let's do it." I punch the power button on the remote. "Let me get some cash." On the way through the kitchen, I jot a note for Tee-tee, in case she gets back before we do:

*Walking to Dollar Shopper. Be back soon. If you come to pick us up, can I drive back home?*

I run upstairs to get my purse and drag the neon pink parka from the back of my closet. I'm downstairs and heading through the kitchen when Nikky's scrawl at the bottom of the note catches my eye:

*P.S. Love you, Mom. You're the best. N.*

We set off through the backyard, cross the salted and sanded road, and slide down the roadside gully that borders a wooded area with a cluster of well-kept mobile homes. Christmas lights twinkle in a few windows, and icicle lights—probably there since last Christmas—hang from eaves. Shrubs are encased in wire cages or wrapped in burlap to keep hungry deer from demolishing them.

The thin layer of ice-crusted snow crunches under our feet as we move through the woods, pushing aside pine boughs. I spot a bathtub-sized circular area, cleared of snow down to dried leaves, and crouch next to it.

"Look, Nik. I'll bet deer have been bedding here." Black scat dots the snow. Deer tracks lead off in all directions.

Nikky wrinkles his nose. "They're pooping near their bed. How gross is that?"

We set off again. The low sun breaks from behind a cloud and blinds me for an instant. Behind the woods Sandore's field is a trackless expanse of white, edged with crumbling stone walls that once marked off old farm fields. The snow is ankle deep here and blown into wavy drifts along an outcropping of rocks. I reach down and try packing a snowball, but the snow is too fluffy and dry. The snowball disintegrates

in my mitten.

My mood lightens. It's been weeks since I've walked farther from my house than the corner bus stop. The trees under their dusting of snow change from bare maples and oaks to pine. The air smells of wet bark. An occasional gust of wind stings my nose and cheeks, and my breath clouds on each exhale. I'm as buoyant and cheerful as a mountaineer about to ascend Mt. Everest, with the plight of deer the furthest thing from my mind.

"I'm really getting sick of you and Mom arguing all the time." Nikky pushes aside a snow-dusted pine bough, and it sweeps back on me. A mist of fine snow sprays my face.

"Geez, Nik. Watch it." I lick the wet off my lips and maneuver around the prickly bough. "We don't argue *all* the time."

"It seems like all the time to me. I don't know why you're giving her such a hard time about some mangy old deer."

I keep my mouth shut and my thoughts to myself. I'm not up for any more griping. I take a deep breath and plunge ahead through the snow. Gusts of fine granules swirl around us. With Nikky leading the way, we track down a steep slope, round a big rock, and climb over a fallen tree. Dollar Shopper's blue-and-yellow

sign glints in the distance. The parking lot is full of shoppers getting a jump on their Christmas shopping.

Then we hear it.

A sneeze.

Nikky draws a quick breath. I nudge him, and put a finger to my lips. *Ssshhh*, I hiss softly. A squirrel scampers across a springy branch, sifting powdery snow on our heads.

After a few silent moments, I whisper, "Maybe we'd better head back."

Nikky nods. Panic fills his eyes. We both step backward, retracing our tracks a few paces. Before we can turn, we hear it again.

*"Choo."*

Not a high ladylike sneeze, but a loud deep discharge. Then a grunt, and a dull *thunk*. He seems to be within a stand of small pines about twenty yards away.

"Hunter," Nikky whispers. "We'd better warn him we're here or we're dead meat."

For once I think Nikky makes an excellent point. "Hey," I call out. "Humans here."

A rifle-shot *crack* echoes across the valley.

I drop to the ground, yanking Nikky down with me.

"Don't shoot, stupid," Nikky hollers. "We're humans."

Silence. Only the rise and fall of my breath, the blood thudding in my ears and chest. Why isn't he answering?

I can't think straight. Should we run or hide? If we run we might be mistaken for prey. If we hide we might get frostbite waiting for whoever it is to leave. Tee-tee might have a coronary if she can't find or phone us. My cell is still where I left it Friday night. On the kitchen counter.

I lift my head, my eyes level with the snow. No more sneezes. Just green pines with brown trunks and white snow and . . .

A patch of red moving toward us.

The sneezer trudges out, ducking his head as he steps under pine boughs. Not an orange-vested, middle-aged hunter, but a boy about my age.

"Who's there?" he croaks in a raw, raspy voice. A cough wracks his shoulders.

He's thin, with a sharp angular face. His jeans hang loosely off his hips, bagging a little at the bottom over his construction-worker boots. He looks cold wearing only a flannel shirt under a sleeveless down vest. Snowdrops glisten on his shoulders, in his close-cropped dark hair.

The boy swings something heavy and metal, flashing silver. A panicky thought hits me. *He has a gun.*

154

"Don't shoot," Nikky yells, scrabbling backward across the snow on his belly.

The boy seems confused. "With this?" He holds up a hammer in his left hand, not a gun.

"We heard a shot." I get to my feet and dust snow off my jeans. I keep my eyes on him in case he's a shyster, a scammer, smooth on the outside and slimy on the inside. To my knowledge guys don't hang around in the woods toting hammers, unless they're out to bash something—or someone. A hammer in the grip of a psycho is as deadly as a gun. The guests at Philoxenia House have taught me that.

But he merely coughs into his hand, then rasps, "I hit a pine knot. They explode when you do that. Split the damn tree trunk."

Nikky picks himself up off the snow. "Jeez, you scared us, man. We thought it might be hunters. But hunters don't hunt with hammers, so you can't be one. Unless you're going to bash the deer over the—"

"I'm Darya, this is Nikky." I cut Nikky off before he gets fired up. No sense irritating a stranger armed with a heavy tool. "We live over the hill in the Morningside area."

Hammer Boy doesn't smile, doesn't introduce himself. He swipes a flannelled arm across his runny nose. He looks feverish, his eyes glassy

155

and haunted. But his complexion is the creamy color of café au lait, of chilled milk swirled into hot coffee, a golden summer tan. I could drink in that smooth hot skin . . .

But instead I try being congenial, neighborly, putting him at ease the way we do with agitated guests at Philoxenia House, all the while mortified that my orangey-pink parka shouts *flamingo*, and Nikky's a walking orange traffic cone. Just two clowns frolicking in the woods. "We're headed over to Dollar Shopper." I grasp Nikky's gloved hand and drag him forward. "So we'll just be on our way. We'd normally drive, but the roads are slick." I avoid mentioning that I couldn't drive even if the roads weren't slick. Not that I care what he thinks, but something inside me wants to impress him with the fact that I'm not a child. Or a clown.

"You're trespassing on my uncle's property," he growls through gritted teeth. He sounds stuffed up, congested, like he has the flu or a really bad head cold. I don't want to go anywhere near him, a germ incubator.

Nikky pipes up. "You mean Mr. Sandore? He's your uncle?"

Hammer Boy starts to say something, but before he can speak a coughing fit takes him. He swings the hammer in a broad arc as if to

frighten us off.

"Understood. We're trespassing on your uncle's property. We won't cross your precious land again." I swallow hard, close to choking on those words. I want to ask him why he's being such a jerk. Instead, I spit out a threat. "Unless Dollar Shopper buys it up for a parking lot."

His eyes lighten briefly, the corners of his lips turning up slightly. Then his face resumes its glower. "Fat chance." He turns and walks to the *Posted* sign tacked to a nearby oak. With the claw end of the hammer, he rips the poster off the tree.

"Hey, don't do that." I slog through the snow toward him, stopping a few feet away. "Leave those signs up." I want to pelt him with a snowball, one with a chunk of ice in the center.

He turns around, hammer raised. He doesn't look directly at me, but keeps his eyes focused on the trees behind me. "What's it to you? My uncle wants them down."

"Without the *Posted* signs, your uncle's land will be open to hunters. They'll kill the deer."

"That's the whole point." He turns and sneezes, then reaches into his vest and pulls out a yellow paper with hand-printed lettering. Holding the paper up against the same tree, he tacks it with his hammer, top and bottom.

Jacqueline Horsfall

I move in for a closer look. My heart
plummets.

The big black letters read:

# HUNTERS WELCOME

After dinner, Tee-tee rattles open the Sunday paper. "Well, look at this!" She folds the paper and slides it toward me. "The town board has submitted a proposal to allow farmers special hunting privileges to shoot deer on their land out of season."

I read the column:

"Of farmers listing wildlife damage as a major concern, most said deer are the worst culprits. Statewide, deer damage costs farmers about sixty million dollars."

I look up at Tee-tee. "And that means—"

"Farmers may kill as many deer as they want. In fact, they're encouraged to do just that. To cut back the deer population, which the D. E. E. R. resolution supports."

Cold prickles march up my spine. "But the deer will be safe in our yard, right? Hunters and farmers can't hunt on our land."

"That's right, they can't hunt in residential areas, near homes, or on posted land."

It pops out of Nikky's mouth before I can shush him. "Our neighbor's taken down his *Posted* signs."

*Uh-oh.* My stomach takes a nosedive. Back home before Tee-tee, I'd tossed the note and made Nikky swear not to tattle on us.

Tee-tee sips her coffee, studying us over the top of her bifocals. "Who's that?"

I have to shoulder the blame now that Nikky has blabbed. "Sandore. Nikky and I had a run-in with his nasty nephew this afternoon. He was posting *Hunters Welcome* signs on their property." True, but not too much detail.

Tee-tee folds her arms across her chest and glares at me. "I thought I told you it's not safe to cut across fields in deer hunting season. In fact, I forbid it."

"But we didn't cut through. I needed some exercise—like you did this morning—and Nikky didn't want me to go alone. We only walked as far as the edge of Sandore's field."

Tee-tee smiles at Nikky and tousles his hair. "Taking care of your sister, huh? You're my fella."

Nikky tries out the big word. "Tress-passing. That's what the mean boy with hammer said we were doing. He said Mr. Sandore is his uncle, and we were tress-passing."

"Don't take it personally, kids. Anyone who puts up with Ramon Sandore has a good reason to turn nasty." Tee-tee chuckles. "That soft-hearted old coot. I'd heard he'd taken in a relative." She leans toward me and digs her nails into my arm. "And a reminder, sweetie, although Lord knows

it's too late for a warning now. Do. Not. Cross. Fields. During. Hunting. Season." She raises her eyebrows at me. "Got it?"

"Yeah, yeah," I say, putting her off. "So maybe we can draw the deer to our property instead, to protect them now that Sandore has turned traitor."

Tee-tee shakes her head, clacking her cup down hard on the saucer. "But you *know* I don't want deer here. We've already had this discussion. Why do you think I've been trying to discourage them with repellents? Why did I forbid you to feed the deer?" Her look is firm, unyielding. "Answer me, please."

"Because we're not running a deer yard," I murmur.

"Exactly." Tee-tee's face softens a little. "It's not that I totally agree with the town resolution. I don't like the idea of killing defenseless creatures either."

"They *are* defenseless. They can't shoot back."

"But the deer population has doubled in the past few years. The number of new hunters is actually declining. Men don't hunt for sport anymore."

I pop forward in my chair. "That's good."

"Good and bad," Tee-tee says, pushing

161

back from the table. "Like everything else in this world. But no matter how beautiful and defenseless these creatures are, I still don't want deer destroying our property. Understand?"

"But they're *hungry*. And *unarmed*."

"Deer have other ways of protecting themselves. Continually moving. Feeding in posted deer yards. Even attacking humans."

"Deer attack humans?" I can't believe it. No way are those gentle grazing creatures dangerous.

"Just last month a buck gored a farmer in the chest, using its antlers. The buck had been in rut, the breeding cycle, when they're very aggressive."

"The farmer's okay, right?"

Tee-tee slices a hand across her neck. "Killed him. So much for unarmed deer."

I try another tactic. "So why can't we feed them deer food? Maybe we could drop off some fruit at the edge of our property. Or set up a salt lick. Deer love salt, right?"

"That will just help them breed more," Tee-tee says firmly. "And the more deer there are, the more competition for food." She takes her cup to the sink. "Think about this, Darya. Lots of deer are hit by cars every year. Some die instantly, but some run off injured to die painful deaths

later on. Isn't it better for hunters to kill them with one clean, painless shot?"

I trace a circle with my spoon in the congealed gravy on my plate. Bulls-eye. The deer have only three options: shot, starved, or rammed by a truck.

"This is so unfair," I shout.

"Yes, it is," she says. "But no one ever said life is fair."

"But why?"

"There isn't any *why*, Darya."

"Yes, there is. Why can't people learn that killing isn't the answer to everything that spoils their lifestyle? Why can't we protect deer?"

"We can't," Tee-tee says.

"You mean *you* can't."

"That's right. *I* can't. And I won't."

While Tee-tee loads the dishwasher, I tie up the kitchen trash bag and carry it outside to the cans, like Cinderella for her evil stepmother. The snow lies in wind-driven ripples against the foundation, against the thick bases of the shrubs. I walk once around the house, searching for deer tracks. None. Silently I pray for the deer to find a hidden shelter, away from people, away from D. E. E. R.

When I step back inside, Tee-tee is sponging

163

off the counter. "I know you mean well, Darya, but sometimes your head is in the clouds." Tee-tee smiles as she says this, but it's obvious she thinks I'm a starry-eyed dreamer. Adopt a child you don't want, and you just might get stuck with a freak who thinks dumb animals are worth rescuing.

*The buck plunges through the brush, his breath coming in deep gasps, his tongue protruding from the side of his mouth. Several times he slips, falls on his side.*

*An explosion. A hot, searing pain strikes his left shoulder, slicing through tendon and muscle. The impact knocks him to his knees.*

*Zing! A bullet ricochets off a boulder less than a step away, whining like an insect.*

*The buck struggles to his feet and stands for a second, then staggers sideways.*

*Zing! A bullet sings through the span of his antlers, and he shakes his head as if plagued by bees.*

*Zing!* Lightning dances before his eyes, and the top fork of his left antler drops to the ground. Crazed with fright and pain, he lunges up the hillside and crashes down the other side. He slows at the bottom and stands swaying, so weak that his muzzle almost touches the ground.

# MATRYOSHKA

*Ants in my pants. Head in the clouds.*

On the plane from Russia to America, I sat balled up on the seat next to the window, my hands cupped over my eyes, peeking through the slits between my fingers.

I was even higher than our room in the Hotel Moskva.

Nikky snoozed on Tee-tee's lap, held by a harness strapped to her body.

I squirmed against my seatbelt, plucking at the metal buckle. With a clack it opened, and I popped forward to press my nose against the window.

Tee-tee tugged me back into my seat.

*"Ostav'te menja,"* I cried, bouncing back to the window.

When Tee-tee tugged me back again, I turned and swatted at her arm. She lifted a hand. I thought she would slap me, but she was only signaling to the flight attendant for help.

*"Stoy. Stoytyee toot."* I rapped on the window and pleaded. Why didn't she understand that I had to do this?

But Tee-tee couldn't speak Russian, and I spoke no English. Even our sign language was misinterpreted.

Finally a businessman across the aisle leaned over and spoke quietly to Tee-tee, then to me in my own language.

"Sit down and be quiet," he told me. "The plane cannot stop here. You cannot get off and walk on the clouds."

After we landed in New York City, Tee-tee rushed us through customs and bundled us into her car. In the backseat was a soft navy-blue upholstered car seat for Nikky. For me, the Unexpected Child, nothing. Tee-tee buckled me into the seat and drew the strap under my arm. That way, if we were in an accident, I might lose an arm but not my head.

Out of her purse came Nikky's yellow duck wearing its Yankees' cap. Nikky crushed it in his arms and jiggled with joy in his seat, his new

Baby Gap sneakers kicking the air. She reached into her purse again, fished around for a moment, then pulled out a hand-size wooden doll painted in red, yellow, green, and black.

My matryoshka doll. The one I'd had with me at the orphanage. The one my birth mother had played with as a girl, and her mother before her. I pressed it to my chest, tugging at and twisting the smooth wooden surface. Tee-tee again misinterpreted my anguished cries and whimpering words of love for this doll, so she yanked it from my hands and turned it around and over, looking for splinters, loose nails, anything that might pinch or stick me. I grabbed at my doll. I howled and shrieked as we wrestled with it in a tug of war. In brotherly sympathy Nikky's cooing turned to hitched sobbing, then to red-faced screaming. Finally Tee-tee blew out a weary breath and dropped the doll into my lap. She got behind the wheel and turned the radio up full blast.

The loud music calmed me. I grasped the doll's head and foot, and twisted hard. The head and foot separated, and a smaller identical doll fell into my lap, one that had been hidden inside.

Two for the price of one, just like me and Nikky.

I pulled the second doll apart. Another doll, identical to the first two, but smaller, fell out.

Inside the third doll was a mini doll, about the size of my thumb. It didn't twist open.

Quadruplet dolls, one inside of the other, like an onion. Peel off one layer and another appears underneath, until the true center is reached.

Where is my true center? Who is the real me? Tee-tee wants me to be a normal teenager, but what is normal? If it's being a robot, following orders, doing things just because it's the status quo, then I don't do normal. On a certain level, I'm a brat. Tell me not to do something, and I'll do it ten times more.

Sometimes now I open the doll and remove each inner one, lining them up in a row. It makes me feel closer to my mother.

My *real* mother. The one who wanted me.

# Deer murderer

**F**alse alarm. No snow day. Only a couple of inches fell overnight, not enough for canceling school, even though the TV weather hottie was all worked up and the road crews were on standby. Mother Nature and Tee-tee could be twin sisters, they're both so ridiculously unpredictable. If I see a storm brewing on Tee-tee's face, I get all outfitted in my foul-weather gear and hip boots, ready for a battering. Then she surprises me with a rainbow.

Like this morning when she got up early to make me French toast with sourdough bread and real maple syrup—which is to die for, but so expensive she only buys it for Easter—boogying around the kitchen and singing along with the

Classic Rock FM station as though nothing had happened between us last night.

I stuff my coat in my locker, bang it shut, and trot down the hall just as the first bell rings. I join the herd sluicing through the homeroom door, a noisy but friendly bunch, my classmates. I've known most of them since kindergarten, so there's none of that cliquey, snobbish garbage that I've heard goes on in big-city schools. It's impossible to be haughty or pompous when everyone remembers how you peed your pants on the first day of second grade or earned a time out for picking your nose and wiping the boogers under your desk.

As we bunch up at the door, a vinyl binder pokes my back and someone grunts *sorry* close to my ear. His breath reeks of garlic and onions—a stomach-churner first thing in the morning—and I'm positive it's Farique Azuli who, I'm told, has a mad crush on me. He's a sweet braniac, but I wish he'd switch to granola for breakfast instead of Moong Dal. I squeeze past the bodies circling Mrs. Nolan's desk, drop my pack on the floor, and slide into my seat. Just another Manic Monday.

The desk in front of mine has been empty for a few weeks. The friendly girl who sat there disappeared with her family when a *Foreclosure*

sign replaced the *For Sale* sign in their yard. But today an unfamiliar head with cropped dark hair blocks my view.

No, it can't possibly be. *Hammer Boy.*

I slouch down, praying he won't turn around. I have no reason to talk to him again, or ever, for that matter. He reaches a hand up and scratches the top of his head. At least he isn't armed with a shop tool.

He tips his chair back, stretches both arms, and yawns. The chair slips down with a *thunk* and hits my desk. "Sorry," he says, shooting a glance over his shoulder.

I lower my head and tent a hand over my brow, pretending to be deep in thought. Maybe he won't recognize me in my street clothes, sans clown parka.

No such luck. His head whips around. His eyes narrow. "Oh, it's you. The trespasser," he says with a smirk. "The Russian spy." His voice is still hoarse and gravelly, but I now detect a syncopated rhythm, like in those TV ads for exotic tropical beach vacations.

I lift a pinkie finger and take him in. He wears a faded short-sleeved T-shirt with a sagging neckline, despite the fact that our classroom is as cold as a meat locker on Mondays.

He dips his head, peers at me under my

shield, and taps my hand with his pencil. "It *is* you, isn't it? The spy on my uncle's property?"

I reach into my pack for my books and day planner, and slam them down on my desk. "I am *not* a spy. And what's the big deal if I *am* Russian? Everybody in this country comes from somewhere else." The fact that I've lived in New York since kindergarten doesn't seem to click with some people. Their thinking is: Once an outsider, always an outsider.

He scoots his chair sideways and swivels his body to face me. He props his taut, bare, goose-bumpy forearms on my desk. I have a sudden urge to offer him my sweater. He must be freezing. A spasm overtakes him, and he turns his head and coughs into the crook of an elbow. He sucks for a moment, and the air sweetens with the fruity scent of a cherry cough drop. My eyes stray to his full lips, and away again. I hope he hasn't noticed. It's a powerful reflex I'm trying to control, the way my eyes zero in on a guy's lips, gauging the kissability factor. I always assumed this personal flaw applied only to guys I liked, but now it's obviously happening with guys I detest too.

He picks up a book from my desk and squints at the title. "Poetry?" He flips a few pages, feigning interest, then snaps the book shut. "You

really read this stuff on your own? Not for extra credit?"

I snatch the book from his hand. I've entirely given up on the idea of not losing my temper. "A Russian spy who reads contemporary American poetry." I widen my eyes in mock amazement. "How bizarre is *that*?" Heads swivel in our direction as my voice ratchets up. "I surrender. You've found me out. I'm obviously a terrorist plotting to bomb our library's poetry acquisitions." At the end of this rant, I'm panting, not from anger, but from holding back.

Mrs. Nolan looks up from her paper-swamped desk and points a finger at me, mouthing *OK*? I nod enthusiastically and crack the fakest grin ever.

He leans forward. His face close to mine, too close, blocking out the teacher. Fever-heat radiates from his skin, and I now understand why he's wearing a flimsy T-shirt instead of a fleece pullover. It all makes sense. The goose bumps, the fever. He should be in bed fighting the flu, not fighting with me.

He soothes me with a cherry-scented whisper. "Take it easy. I'm kidding."

I can't take my eyes off his mouth, his large white teeth. I crave more of his sweet breath.

He whispers again, "Easy, my Queen."

*My Queen?* Have I heard right? The fluorescent lights above us flicker and buzz, flicker and buzz, as if the ballast starter is cutting out. The buzzing reminds me of a swarm, of a spiraling tower of bees.

He wrenches around in his chair and drops his head over the edge of his desk. *Choof, choof.* The sneeze is loud and mucousy. I tap him on the shoulder and offer a tissue. He turns to me again, his red-rimmed eyes glistening. I like his eyes. They're dark brown without flecks of gold or any other color. They remind me of deer eyes. I think it would be a mistake to tell him *your eyes remind me of deer*, but I find the thought reassuring. He has unusually long lashes for a guy and . . . something else.

It hits me now. I know those eyes. I know that voice, that sneeze. I need only to close my mind and fall all over again into that lucid dream. The memory is dazzling.

*Yes, my Queen?*

*Rah. Rah-Lee.*

He waves a hand in front of my face. "Earth to Russky. You okay? I didn't spray you, did I?" He shoots the balled-up tissue toward the teacher's wastebasket. Score.

"You seem . . . familiar somehow." I notice a small cut where he's nicked himself shaving,

and an angry red pimple on his chin. Very un-deer-like, I think smugly.

He seems to give this some serious thought. "Maybe we knew each other in another life," he says finally.

It's out before I can clamp it. "And I probably hated you then too."

His mouth gapes in genuine surprise. This time I've really hurt him. I could kick myself.

"You hate me? What did I do?" He avoids my eyes. "You don't even know me."

"I wish . . ." I don't know what I wish. I wish I could go home and die.

"Because I called you a spy? Because I obeyed my uncle? That's why you hate me?"

"I don't hate you!" In my throat is the whole sentence: *I think I love you.* Before I can help it, my eyes stray to his lips again. I silently curse and tear my gaze away. I want to karate chop him, not kiss him.

I press back in my seat and force my eyes to sweep the room. My classmates turn away, murmuring, embarrassed at being caught in the act of eavesdropping. We're still on the teacher's radar as she grades papers. She shoots us piercing stares over the top of her glasses, a stern owl scrutinizing her forest. I rummage around in my pack for pens, gum, anything to

keep my hands busy and eyes averted.

He seems unaware that, for me anyway, the conversation is terminated, finito. "My uncle says you're adopted by that old single lady who runs the service for sleaze-bags."

That does it. I leap up from my chair and slap my palms on the desk. "She's not an old lady." The room hushes to silence. Mrs. Nolan's heels click down the floor toward us. "And she helps people—people, not sleaze-bags—in crisis, no matter if they're rich or poor."

The corners of his mouth lift in that hint of a smile. "So she might help me? *If* I had a crisis, I mean?" I think he's mocking me, but I'm not sure.

"*Bet* on it," I spit out, close to snarling. "She'll lock you up in the nuthouse for hammer-toting psychotics who slaughter wildlife." Mrs. Nolan grips my arm, urging me back down to my seat.

"Whoa," he says, hands up in surrender. "Peace, Russky." He grins at the teacher, twists around in his chair, and scoots it forward, away from me.

He will not spoil my good day. My attention's on the board, ignoring him, noting next week's vacation schedule. "DEER MURDERER," I write in bold black letters in my notebook with a blood-red pen, pressing so hard I nearly tear

through the paper. I draw poison-tipped arrows aimed his back. Each arrow drips crimson blobs, his blood.

After announcements, Mrs. Nolan introduces Hammer Boy to the class as "Rawley Sandore, our new student from St. Thomas, one of the Virgin Islands." She moves to an elongated wall map of our globe and points to the Caribbean. A finger of small islands lay clustered in a hook between North and South America, close to the equator, known as the West Indies.

I roll his name around on my tongue. Rawley. It has a familiar ring. *Raw*-ley. Raw-*ley*.

*Rah-Lee.*

The room spins. I grasp the edges of my desk and try not to be sick. A coincidence. Just a weird coincidence, that's all.

Rawley's *choof* explodes across the room. It's clear now why he's sick and dressed for summer. He's probably got a suitcase full of cargo shorts, tank tops, and flip-flops. He's accustomed to hammering palms instead of pines. Killing dolphins instead of deer.

My eyes move from the Caribbean across the Atlantic to the broad expanse of Mother Russia. I measure the distances, counting lines of latitude and longitude. Although we come from opposite sides of the globe, Rawley is as far from

his true home as I am from mine. As much as I hate to admit it, he and I are peas in a pod. Two strangers. Two outsiders.

Throughout the day we're in many of the same classes. I'm intrigued by his casual sprawl, his dark head thrown back, work boots cocked outward in the aisles, gigantic leather barriers. They look big enough to be his uncle's boots, and probably are.

He sits directly in front of me in English because the teacher prefers alphabetical seating, Sandore before Tomasio. Between snatches of teacher drone, I catch wafts of something clean and fresh like baby shampoo. Why haven't I noticed this before? He probably showered after gym class—but with baby shampoo in a locker room full of guys? Is he that confident?

But the larger question is this: How could anyone who smells so sweet—of babies and cherries—be such a jerk?

Final bell. I linger at my desk for a while, letting the room clear, before heading to my locker. I twirl the dial. A finger taps my shoulder.

"Hey, Russky." Rawley leans casually against the lockers and tips his head sideways as if assessing me. His eyes gleam jet, feral under his

long lashes. "You're right. I was out of line this morning." He makes a quick bow at the waist. "My most humble apologies, my lady."

I turn my back to him and jerk at my coat, its loop twisted around the hook in my locker.

"I read your letter in the paper this morning. My uncle showed me."

*Damn.* I was hoping for a few days to get my story straight in my head. The curse of cyberspace, so speedy that you're in the spotlight as soon as you hit SEND.

"So what's this fixation with deer?" He pushes my arm aside, lifts my coat off the hook, and shakes it open for me. I hesitate for an instant, then slip my arms through. As he tugs the collar up, he touches my neck lightly and runs his finger over the tiny arc of bone at my nape.

I bite my lip. Blood whooshes in my ears.

"Tag," he rumbles. "Your tag's sticking up."

"Oh." I lose my train of thought. That café au lait complexion. That drinkable skin.

"The deer. How come you're so steamed over them?"

I huff out a breath, shoulder my pack, and slam my locker shut. I'm shaking. I want to get away, to get out of here before I make a fool of myself. "They're cute. I like them. They're not hurting anyone. End of story."

I push past him and start down the hall, but he circles me and walks backwards as he talks to me. "No, really, I want to know."

I stop and glare at him. He's solemn now, still and watchful. We stand in the middle of the hall, an island of two, while classmates flow around us. Except Farique, who stands motionless near the office door, his fists clenched. He seems tensed-up, ready to pounce on Rawley. He stares for a moment, then drops his gaze to the floor.

"They have the same right to live as anyone else."

Rawley shrugs. "Maybe. My uncle calls them nuisance animals, like rodents. Rats on stilts. They eat his crops. He hit a deer last month. Got a bum leg and a big repair bill because of it."

"Oh, sorry to hear—"

"And that's why he's allowing hunters on his land."

"Well, of course not everyone agrees. Even Tee-tee thinks—"

"Why don't you call her Mom?"

"What?" An unexpected punch to the gut. I'm stunned at the personal question.

"Your *Tee-tee*, as you call her. Why don't you call her Mom? She adopted you, right?"

I launch into my usual spiel. "You see, her name's Teresa Tomasio, so people call her Tee-

182

tee, like her initials." I draw two air *T*s with my finger. "T. T."

"Yeah, yeah, my uncle told me all that." Rawley shifts his weight and glances in Farique's direction. A smile plays over his face. I can tell he's enjoying this.

"You didn't answer my question. Why don't *you* call her Mom?"

*Because she's not.*

My throat clogs up. How could he possibly understand? How could I explain to a complete stranger that my birth mother was my *real* mother, someone who wanted me for me, not someone who adopted me only because I came with the baby.

I hear buses rev up, ready to motor out of the circle.

"It's none of your damned business." I shove him out of the way and charge toward the door. Before I've gone six strides, Farique is at my side, gripping my elbow. I twist away and take the stairs two at a time.

"See you tomorrow, Russky!" Rawley growls at me. A sudden explosive sneeze follows me out the door.

The bus grinds to a stop at my corner, and the red STOP hexagon lifts away from the

driver's side. Traffic comes to a halt—traffic I desperately wish to be a part of again, and soon, in my own energy-efficient hybrid. But at this point I'll settle for anything with four tires, a halfway decent radio, and an air bag. I scratch this afternoon as a driving opportunity. Not going to happen. A coworker's bound to have given Tee-tee a heads-up about my letter to the newspaper. Rawley's aggravation will be nothing compared to her rage. At least I'll have time to smother my sorrows in some leftover pizza before she gets home from work.

The afternoon is mild. The roads are wet, the snow melting on lawns, exposing green patches. Water drips from roofs with a *tik-tik-tik* sound. As the bus motors off, my coat flaps open, and my hair lifts in the breeze. I take a deep breath and hold the sharp aroma of fresh pine inside, then exhale all my pent-up frustrations from the day. To ready myself for tonight.

A minivan speeds by and sends a heavy spray of slush toward me. I dance back from the splatter and yell at the driver. It feels great to take my rage out on an anonymous person who can't sass me back and doesn't care one whit about who my mother is or why I like deer.

In the mudroom I shed my coat and heavy-

soled shoes, and slip into my house clogs. "Anybody here?" I figure Nikky will have beaten me home.

Instead, Tee-tee steps inside, closes the door, and leans against it. She's breathing fast, her eyes puffy and red-rimmed.

Oh god, has she been crying?

"Tee-tee, I'm really sorry I didn't tell you about the—"

"Libby's back," she whispers, putting a finger to her lips, "and she's hurt. When the police called, I left work early and met them here." I detect a note of fear in Tee-tee's voice.

"Daytime isn't safe," I hiss at her. "And Jax might know of this place. He might have beaten it out of her."

"They drove Libby and the kids in a supply company's delivery van. They had no choice. The other county homes are full up."

"But we still don't have a security system."

Tee-tee rubs her forehead with both hands.

"And Home Fix-it hasn't replaced the patio door yet. We're wide open for attack." She's stressed out, and I'm not helping. "Okay, okay." I give her a quick hug. "We'll double-check the locks tonight."

Her face visibly relaxes. "And keep the floodlights on all night."

Like a couple hundred-watt bulbs will keep a psycho away—but I don't say that.

"And maybe nail that big sheet of plywood over the door. The one from Nikky's old skateboard ramp."

That's my girl. She's back to being take-charge Tee-tee again.

"So how's Libby?"

"She's in pretty bad shape. A broken arm this time. He shoved her down a flight of stairs. After he'd slammed her fingers in the car door. She also has some uterine bleeding."

*And she'll probably forgive him again*, I nearly say. For better or worse is one marriage vow I'll never utter. I scoop up my books and paste on a fake smile as we make our way into the kitchen. "I hope we're doing the right thing," I mutter to myself.

Maddie and Nikky are sitting at the table, paper and crayons jumbled on top. I toss my books on the counter and slide into a chair next to them.

Nikky looks up from his math homework. "Libby went upstairs. I carried Ethan for her."

"Thanks, Nikky-babe," Tee-tee says.

"And *pee-you*." He pinches his nose. "I changed his diaper."

Tee-tee circles her arms around him and

plants a wet smooch on his cheek. "You're the best boy in the whole world. I'm so lucky to have the illustrious Master of Poopypants as my son."

"Poopypants," Maddie squeals.

"Geez, Mom, cut it out." Nikky flinches and wrenches away, but I know he loves the attention.

A trace of envy sneaks into my head, a mere sliver. I stifle it immediately.

"See my dinosaur." Maddie pushes a crumpled paper toward me. "A Ty-ran-sore."

"She means Tyrannosaurus Rex," Nikky butts in. "I'm teaching her the scientific words."

I smile at the brown-crayoned drawing of a monstrous blob eating what looks to be a stick-figure reindeer. Santa is falling off his sleigh, in fright, I suppose.

"Scary." I pretend to shiver. I reach over to smooth her hair. For a moment, with all of us at the table, I'm able to kid myself, to pretend that it's a normal day—and that the only monsters in the world are blobs and stick figures on construction paper.

Libby stands at the top of the stairs, holding Ethan in her good arm. Her bashed arm is in a sling, bound in a plaster cast from elbow to wrist.

For a split second she teeters on the edge of the landing. Her eyelids flutter, her face drains of color, and her body starts to crumple.

In my mind's eye I see her pass out and tumble down without a free hand to hold the railing. Bumping down the treads, crushing Ethan beneath her. Like one of Tee-tee's clients who was descending the stairs with her four-month-old baby, leading her four older kids, when one stumbled and bumped her from behind. The next thing she knew, she was in midair, flying headfirst down the staircase. Her back slammed hard against the middle steps, and she tumbled down the rest, crashing on top of her infant, shattering both his legs. It all happened in a split second.

I barrel up the stairs, two at a time. "Can I help, Libby?" I grip her good arm to steady her. "Can I help you with Ethan?"

Her head jerks, and she snaps out of her daze. She seems unaware of how close she came to breaking more than an arm. "Oh! Please." She hands Ethan to me.

He stiffens, and his mouth curls into an *O* as he winds up for a howl.

"He needs another diaper change." Libby leads the way back to the guest bedroom. "He has diarrhea." She winces as she rounds the

corner and her wrapped arm bumps against the jamb.

I lay Ethan on the changing table and strip back the diaper tabs. Libby hands me a fresh diaper. I unfold it and then slip it under the soiled one. I could do this in my sleep, considering all the babies who've stayed with us. I powdered Nikky's bottom a few times too, when Tee-tee needed help in the beginning.

Ethan scrunches his eyebrows at me and bats the air, his legs kicking out like a frog's. I lean down and nuzzle his head. He's a cutie, plump and toothless, with a tuft of light hair at his crown. I plan to have my own babies someday. Little cheeks I can kiss, who come through me and yet are not me. Who carry the bloodline of my Russian family. Maybe I'll see my mother's pert nose on my daughter, my father's curly hair and square chin on my son. My parents will come alive through my children.

Or maybe I won't physically have babies. I'll be a successful career woman like Tee-tee, then adopt a few. I have a low pain tolerance. And from those health channel birth shows, I know having a baby is painful and bloody, with lots of screaming and grunting, accompanied by hovering husbands who try to be ultra-helpful with breath-coaching and back-rubbing and

shaved-ice feeding, but seem jittery and helpless and would probably rather be out in the waiting room watching football. Maybe Tee-tee played it smart by adopting us.

Either way, I haven't gotten to that place where my motherly instincts have kicked in yet.

I wonder which was more painful for Libby—childbirth, or being punched in the face? At least in childbirth, she got a prize at the end, a baby who made her forget all her childbirth pains. No prizes come with punches, unless it's a televised boxing match.

I hold my breath, pull back the messy diaper, and separate his legs. Ethan has a wicked case of diaper rash, angry red skin with clear watery blisters. The folds of his tiny penis are caked with dried poop, and a fresh orangey smear tracks up his back.

"I haven't been able to clean him up good," Libby says, her voice shaky. "My arm."

"Whew." The stink is pungent, penetrating, nothing like a breastfed baby's stools should be. "Has Ethan had a well-baby check-up recently?"

Libby shakes her head. "No," she whispers. "I couldn't get out. He wouldn't let me have the car."

I snap a wet wipe out of its plastic container.

I'm trying to remain cool and not say what I'm thinking: *You need some serious spine, girl.*

"I know you told me so," she says, her voice quiet, "and I guess you were right."

"I wish I hadn't been."

Libby tosses back her hair, a haughty gesture. "I know what you think . . . but I wasn't always like this. I was an honor student, fourth in my class. And I was in the show choir. I sang the lead in our senior class musical. The director said I had star potential." She shifts her head and catches her reflection in the dresser mirror. "I was pretty . . ." The words die on her lips. She shakes as if crying, but she's silent.

I use close to a dozen wipes on Ethan's bottom, then goop on some white ointment and smear it over his red bottom and into the creases of his legs.

"You're good at this," Libby says.

"I've had lots of practice." The face of our last guest comes to mind, a pregnant mother with a red slice across her cheek and a fourteen-month-old in her arms. "Is that when you met Jax?" I ask softly.

"He was captain of the hockey team. We hooked up after a game. I was crazy for him. You wouldn't believe the silly stuff we did together. Three afternoons a week we trained for a

marathon. He made s'mores in the microwave. I still have love poems he wrote me, the ones he set to music and played on his guitar. The yearbook labeled us *Beauty and the Beast*. We were an item. And he was there for me when my grandma died." A smile forms on her lips as she remembers, and just as quickly vanishes. "But he was jealous then too. He beat up anyone who looked at me sideways."

"So why did you marry him?" I wait for her to go on, but I'm afraid she might cry.

"I . . . I loved him. I thought his jealousy demonstrated his total love for me." She looks at me with teary eyes. "But I should have paid attention to the big, clanging alarm bells in my head. His total love turned into total bondage."

"Is that why you dropped out of college?" I ball up the messy diaper, heave it into a plastic grocery bag, and side-tab the fresh diaper. Ethan's eyes flick, on the edge of snoozing. I want to know so much. I'm hoping she'll confide in me. I'm curious about why love turns to hate. Or love merges with hate. Does she still love this monster-man who is the father of her children?

"He thought I was cheating on him with one of my professors."

"You weren't, were you?"

"No. My biology professor was helping me

arrange a transfer to a four-year university med program. We had to fill out a lot of paperwork together."

"So you explained this to Jax and—"

"He also couldn't handle the fact that I had guy friends at school. That people can actually be friends with members of the opposite sex."

"So then you stayed home and had Maddie and Ethan?"

"I thought having babies would patch things up between us, that he'd see I really loved only him. But now he's jealous of imagined stuff. That I sneak out to meet a lover. Like I'd be able to manage an affair with two babies. He keeps me prisoner in our house. If I go out, he has to know where I am every second."

"Can't you go out when he goes to work?"

"He takes the car. He says we only need one car."

"That sounds . . . weird," I say, not wanting to freak her out using the word *psychotic*.

"More than weird. If I had to go out at night, for groceries or baby stuff, he'd check my panties when I returned, to make sure they were the same ones I'd left the house in."

"Geez."

Libby snorts a laugh. "Yeah, like I'd have a whole new set at my lover's house."

193

I slip one hand under Ethan's puffy diaper-wrapped bottom and, cradling his head with my other hand, lift him into the crib. He stiffens and squinches up his eyes, but settles down with a binkie. I sit on the bed next to Libby and put an arm around her. She tips her head onto my shoulder. Her lank, tangled hair falls over her face. Her shoulders shake. She reaches for a tissue and blows her nose. "Jax stuffs his frustration in his fists," she says finally, "and when his weapons need release, they find me. Sometimes he can be such a . . ."

*Undeserving jerk.*

". . . puckhead."

Close enough, Libby girl. So I have to ask the question. "Do you still love him?"

Her shoulders shrug. "I don't know. I guess." She pauses. "And deep inside, I know he loves me too. Me and the kids. He just gets in a funk sometimes." She lets out a deep sigh. "Or maybe it's my fault. I get on his back about smoking, about how it isn't good for the kids. I nag him about cleaning up after himself." She runs a finger over her wedding ring, now a symbol of love gone bad. "Yeah, a lot of it is my fault."

Tee-tee's right. What Libby needs is a swift kick in the knickers. How could she defend Jax when he'd whacked her harder than any hockey

puck?

I think about her choices, how one tiny decision changed her life. A decision that probably took only a split second to make. What if she hadn't hooked up with him after the game? Would she be a single university student now, preparing for a medical career?

I wonder how Tee-tee feels about her life choice too. Is she really and truly glad she adopted me? Does she wish it had been only Nikky? Deep down in her heart of hearts, does she think she's made a big mistake after all?

"Do you have a boyfriend, Darya?"

"Not really." Rawley's slurpable complexion shimmers before my eyes. I banish it immediately.

"Good," Libby says, sniffling. "Don't make the same mistake I did."

"I don't plan to." This comes out harsher than I really mean.

*Crash.* Rule Number 4 bites the dust: *The women who stay with us are in no way inferior to us.*

"What I mean is, boys don't interest me much." *Liar.* I've never been the kind of girl who needs a boyfriend. I believe love will find you when you're not looking for it. So I've been actively *not* looking for love. At least this is what

I tell myself.

Libby touches my arm. "It'll be different for you. Someday you'll find a guy who'll treat you right, like a queen."

"I prefer instant gratification." Like Rawley. Like right now. *Easy, my Queen.*

"But you're lucky to have a great mom who cares about you."

"Tee-tee," I remind her.

"Your *mom*," she says, reinforcing the word that I refuse to speak.

"Mommy," Maddie cries from downstairs. "Mommy."

Libby's head jerks up. She dabs at her eyes with the tissue. "Mommy's here, baby," she calls down in a fake-happy voice. "What's wrong?"

"I have to pee-pee," Maddie answers.

"I'll get her." I head for the stairs.

Maddie stands at the bottom in a puddle of pee.

"Tee-tee," I yell toward the kitchen. "Paper towels."

I scoop Maddie up and rush her to the bathroom. I kneel on the floor, soothing her and stripping off her pants. Knuckles rap on the bathroom door. I reach over and crack open the door.

Tee-tee, red-faced and sweaty, stands there

holding a wad of wet paper towels in one hand.

And a folded newspaper in the other.

*Uh-oh. I am dead.*

"What's this about a protest, Darya?" She dumps the paper towels in the wastebasket. "What on earth are you doing, taking on the town board?"

She holds the paper so I can read the caption above my letter:

## Local Student Protests Deer Resolution, Scolds Town Board

It's worse than I thought. "Look, I've given the deer problem a lot of thought. What the trustees are doing is wrong." I try not to whine. Tee-tee hates whining. "The deer are hungry and scared, that's the bottom line."

"The deer aren't the only ones hungry. Many families live on deer meat throughout the year. People are hungry too."

My voice ramps up. "But that's what your Helpline is for. People can use the food pantries."

Tee-tee sighs. "I do understand your viewpoint, but you're getting yourself into a hornet's nest of trouble. The resolution was passed because the community wants to control

the deer population. You're not only fighting the town board but the residents as well."

Maddie's sucks her thumb, swiveling her head from me to Tee-tee and back again as we speak. I scrounge under the sink for a toddler pull-up. Part of me wants to climb inside the cabinet and hole up there until my throat unclenches and I can speak without bawling.

I busy myself with swabbing Maddie's urine-soaked legs and bottom with baby wipes, keeping my watery eyes lowered and talking softly to Maddie until I get my voice under control.

"The deer don't know anything about town boards or resolutions or landscaping," I finally say. "They see the snow and trees and houses, like we do. But they know all kinds of things we don't know, like how to smell danger on the wind and how to find food outside and warm places to sleep. Maybe they have a language we know nothing about. They experience this world different from us, but it's as real to them as it is to us."

"Sweetie, I hear you. I haven't gone over to the Dark Side." Tee-tee thumps her chest. "There's still a smidgen of compassion in this old ticker, believe me." She steadies Maddie as I guide her feet into the pull-up holes. "But it's not smart to take on the town. Besides, it draws attention to

us, and we need to fly below the radar. It's not safe for our guests."

Before Tee-tee can launch into a lecture, the phone rings.

# White nights

*Will you ever marry?*

When I asked Tee-tee this question, she told me the Russian court officials had asked her the same thing. Why, they wanted to know, did a 47-year-old, single American woman want to adopt two children?

How did she plan to support us?

Why did she have no husband?

Was she simply looking for slave labor, children who would cook and clean?

Tee-tee had come prepared with five years' worth of financial statements, proving that she could feed, house, educate not only one child, but two, and wasn't about to sell us on the black market for profit.

Here's what they didn't ask her: *Can you love them both?*

My background was a mystery. With no living relatives to take us in, Nikky and I were a drain on the system. We were expendable.

With enough money, anything is for sale. Even children.

*Stranger in a Strange Land.* I read this book by Robert A. Heinlein last year, mostly because the title spoke to me. The worn paperback was wedged into the corner of Tee-tee's bookcase. The story is about a human raised on Mars, then returned to Earth. No one understands his weird ways, and the government tries to take advantage of him. In the margins Tee-tee had written notes like *we are one* and *love is all.*

Is that where she got her idea for Philoxenia House, the love of strangers?

I, too, am a stranger in a strange land. America is my adoptive home, but will I ever feel totally comfortable here? Tee-tee told me all Americans came from somewhere else, their ancestors immigrants from Europe or Asia or Africa, either in slavery or for religious freedom or for the lure of instant wealth. Her own grandparents arrived here from Sicily in the early 1900s, tired of the drudgery of sulfur

mining, searching for streets paved with gold, as they were led to believe. Tee-tee says she's just as much a stranger in this land as I am.

But at least she knows her parents and remembers her grandparents.

Here's what I remember:

One midsummer day—I am probably four or five—my parents and I drive north to St. Petersburg for White Nights, when the sun never sets but hovers over the horizon. Daylight lasts all day long, even into the hours when it should be night. Papa parks the car, removes the windshield wipers, and carries them with him into the hotel. If he leaves them on the car, they will be stolen before morning.

After dinner and a stroll, hand-in-hand, along the Neva River with throngs of families taking advantage of the lengthened daylight, we return to our room. Papa uncaps a bottle of *vodkah* and pours the clear liquid into two tumblers. He hands one to my mother, and they clink glasses. Papa downs his in one gulp and sets the glass down with a firm *clunk*. Mama leans back in her chair and sips from her glass. Her bare feet rest on the mattress, her ankles crossed. I run my hand up and down her long smooth leg, a dancer's leg. Her toes are misshapen and calloused from years of performing in ballet shoes.

As they drink and speak in low whispers, I doze, for only a moment it seems, then jerk awake. Sunlight streams through the blinds. Music blares over bursts of raucous laughter.

Mama leans over and jiggles my arm. "Are you awake, Darya?"

"What's wrong? Is it time to get up?"

A mischievous smile crinkles her face. "It's midnight. Let's go out and dance."

Papa leads the way as he shoulders through a mob of revelers with their arms hooked, rocking back and forth as they shout-sing with music from a boom box. A balding man in a rumpled business suit leans with one hand against a storefront, head down, vomiting on the pavement at his feet. An empty bottle dangles from his free hand. Two blonde-haired matrons dance a jig, an arm around each other's shoulders, screeching words that might be a song, or a curse. An empty wine bottle clinks as it rolls along the gutter. Everyone is happy that cold and darkness are gone. This is the time to celebrate the heat and light of midsummer, with singing, dancing, and liquor.

Mama steps out into the street, takes both my hands, and swings me in a circle. My feet leave the pavement, and I'm flying, flying with only Mama's hands gripping mine. I shriek

until my face aches. Papa comes to my rescue and sweeps me up. I'm squashed between them as we bounce and grind in a threesome to the throbbing backbeat of a Michael Jackson song.

The music stops, then changes beat. Mama releases me to Papa and steps back. "Watch this, Darya." She lowers herself into a half-crouch and gyrates her hips to the left, swinging her arms to the right. Hips shift right, arms left. She swivels in a gyrating circle, hips and arms in motion. "Baby, come on," she croons with the music, "let's dance the Twist."

More memories from St. Petersburg. The whispery scuff of our paper slippers as we shuffle from room to room through the Hermitage Museum.

"*Dead Stag*," Papa whispers as he squints at the bronze plaque under an oil painting on canvas. I whimper and clutch Mama's hand. In the foreground, close to the right-hand edge of the painting, an antlered stag lies dead in the snow. A snare circles its front hoof. A brown dog sniffs at the stag's haunches while a bearded hunter in a fur-trimmed coat speaks to a turbaned woman holding a baby. Her husband sits nearby, holding a musket. A small girl about Maddie's age, in a red cap and dark apron, looks on, a wondering expression on her face. At the left edge, a boy

in a red cap watches as a man smoking a pipe hones a knife on a sharpening wheel, no doubt to skin the stag. *Kill, kill, kill*, the scene screams at me. *Kill the beast. Slay it. Flay it.*

I hate this painting. I yank Mama's hand and drag her away, down the hall and into the next room filled with paintings of flowers and fruit. She holds me and pats my back, her *shhh* echoing in the high-ceilinged room.

Even then, it seems, I couldn't bear to see deer suffer.

These are the precious fragments of my past, snippets of memories, ones I cling to. If I don't think about them, stamp them into my mind, I'm afraid I'll lose them forever. But questions remain. Who was my father that he could afford the luxury of traveling and staying in a hotel? Tee-tee said he must have been a scientist who was permitted to travel, or a shop owner, who had money to travel.

One thing I'm sure of—my father never abused my mother. And this is how I know: In the Hermitage my parents stand before a painting of a cavalier, clad in red breeches and a black cloak with a white lace ruff around his neck, bending over his reclining lady in a canary yellow gown. He's kissing her lips, his hand resting lightly on her breast. I look up to see Papa's profile

as he glances at Mama, waggling his eyebrows in a lusty leer. Mama giggles and gives him a playful shove. Then he reaches down and pats her bottom.

No, he wouldn't abuse her or be jealous of her admirers. He loved her. I wonder . . . is this the trip when Nikky was conceived?

What happened to my father? My grandparents? Why did they leave me and Nikky at the orphanage? Didn't we have other relatives, aunts and uncles? I wrack my brain for bits of those memories. But there's a void I can't seem to penetrate, no matter how hard I try. They simply aren't there. I'm like a soldier with post-traumatic stress disorder who's experienced a trauma but buries it so deeply that it can't be recovered, except in nightmares.

Maybe Rawley was right. Maybe I'm descended from a family of spies away on secret espionage missions, stirring up trouble.

Stirring up trouble as I am now.

# Let it be

I answer the phone on the third ring.

"Philoxenia?" The voice is low, whispery.

"Yes," I reply, "how many?"

Seconds pass. A faint buzz hisses in the background.

"How many?" I ask again.

The line goes dead.

I lock eyes with Tee-tee across the room, Maddie on her hip. "Whoever it was hung up."

Tee-tee rushes over and thrusts Maddie at me. "Give me that phone." She punches in numbers, then taps her fingers on the wall while she waits. "Officer Willcott, please."

This isn't good.

"Frank, it's Teresa. Did you just call here?"

Tee-tee is silent for a few seconds. Maddie squirms in my arms, so I lower her to the floor.

"He knows the code word then." Tee-tee slumps against the wall. "Okay, thanks." She drops the receiver to her side and rubs her temple in a firm circular motion, her eyes squeezed shut.

I take the phone from her and hang it up. "Was it Jax?" I don't wait for an answer. "What'll we do?"

"They're not sure, but it probably was. Libby must have overheard the code word when they brought her out the first time, and she told him. Or he beat it out of her."

It hits me. She *did* hear it. Friday night when the driver picked me up behind our house. But how could she remember that mouthful of a Greek word? She'd need to have an ear for languages and a good recall.

*I was an honor student, fourth in my class. I was in college too.*

It all makes sense now, although I couldn't see past Libby's beat-up exterior when she first came here. I misjudged her. Libby is one smart cookie. Her bullied, timid outer doll conceals a brainy, clever inner one. It rattles me to think I take people at face value instead of finding out what's inside. I wonder who else I might have

misjudged. The thought makes my brain itch. I think I know the answer. Or answers.

"They're sending a patrol car to keep an eye on our house," Tee-tee assures me. But from the scowl on her face, I can tell she thinks it's hit-or-miss protection.

"Find me," Maddie's voice rings out.

I walk around the sofa calling her name, lifting the cushions, fluffing throw pillows. She's hiding behind the armchair, but I pretend not to see her and walk straight past. "Come out, come out, wherever you are."

Giggles. "You can't find me." More giggles.

I turn swiftly and snatch her up into my arms. She shrieks and kicks her feet. Her small soft hands pat my cheeks, then she dips her head, and plants wet kisses on my face. Happiness washes over me. I can't stop smiling and nuzzling her baby-shampooed hair. Is this what it feels like to be a mother?

"I can't figure out Hammer Boy," I tell Nikky as we dismantle his skateboard ramp in the basement after dinner. Tee-tee said there's no use letting good plywood go to waste when we can use it to reinforce the patio door. "The teachers make a big fuss over him because he's from some virginal island in the Caribbean."

"So what's his real name?" Nikky takes a rubber mallet to the underside of the ramp, but it's a half-hearted swing. He really doesn't want to demolish the ramp because the skateboard park's closed until May, and now he'll have nowhere to practice. How strong his love for Tee-tee must be, that he'd give up his favorite sport just to make her feel safe.

"Something weird. Raw-ley. Probably an island name." I don't know why I say this. My name's pretty weird too. "He seems friendly enough to everybody else. Why is he so nasty to me?"

"Nasty how?"

"In school today he called me a trespasser and a Russian spy. In front of the whole homeroom. And he deliberately infected me with all his germs. He hacked and sneezed right in my face. Can you believe it?"

"Well, we *were* trespassing. And you *are* Russian. And you spy on deer."

I hate it when Nikky puts his own spin on things.

"Maybe because he's sick." Nikky bashes the side supports while I try to keep the contraption from flying across the concrete. My teeth rattle with every *whomp*. "That makes me kinda grouchy too. Especially if I'd have to go out in

a blizzard practically naked and rip posters off trees."

Nikky always sees the best in everybody. He doesn't get riled up and vicious the way I do sometimes. I mumble something about taking a side against your own sister, all the while feeling like a total phony. I'm tired of being a badass. There's a stern disapproving voice in my head that's killing my normally happy buzz. It's a mean, furious voice, like I've angered the gods.

"I'm only saying he doesn't seem so bad. He was sick. And he was out freezing his butt off doing a chore for his uncle. Give the guy a break, Darya."

"I guess. I suppose he could be homesick too."

"Maybe he's scared. I'd be scared too if Mom dumped me on some old fogy relative who lives out in the boonies."

Nikky takes another swing, and his shirtsleeves tighten over taut bumps. My baby brother has muscles. It isn't fair. Babies shouldn't be allowed to grow up. I wish I could freeze Nikky in babyhood with his fat dimpled thighs and bobbing binkie. Is this how all mothers feel when their kids grow up? Libby probably wants Maddie's kisses to belong to her forever, not to some lecherous boy in the future.

"Here's the weird thing, Nik. He seems so familiar to me, like I met him a long time ago. But that's crazy because we're from opposite sides of the globe."

"Everyone has a twin somewhere in the world, that's what Tee-tee says. Maybe you've seen his twin at the mall."

"Not likely. Get this—Rawley thinks we met in another life."

Nikky's eyes light up. "Maybe you were dinosaurs. Rawley was a T-rex who chomped on your butt because you were a plant-eating triceratops."

He's adorable, but if I laugh he'll drive me nuts with the dinosaur stuff.

"Mom said she heard talk at work about him."

This is news to me. "Tee-tee heard something at work about Rawley?"

"Yeah, I think it was about his mom dying. That's why he came to live with his uncle."

*Dying?* I am such an imbecile. His mom is dead. No wonder he's so sensitive about moms. Something had happened to his *one* mom, and I have *two* moms, one I won't even acknowledge. No wonder he made such a big fuss about the *M*-word.

"Could be." Of course it's that. "But he seems

212

to be taking it out on only me."

"It's because you're so bossy. You *did* order him not to take the posters down. Guys don't like bossy girls."

"Being bossy is way better than being rude and nosy."

Nikky lays the mallet on the workbench and picks up a hammer. "So what's he being rude and nosy about?" He hooks the claw end over a nailhead and pulls it with a *screech* from the wood. I'm jolted by the image of Rawley in the woods, a hammer in hand. Boys and their tools.

"He asked me why I didn't call Tee-tee *Mom*. Like it's any of his business."

Nikky stops his nail extraction and looks at me. "So why don't you?"

Now my own brother is ganging up on me too. My jaw clenches, and I barely spit the words out, "Why. Don't. I. *What*?"

"Call her Mom. I really think she'd like that." He stares at me with innocent baby-blues.

"I don't . . . I mean I might—" What am I trying to say? Do I really want Nikky to know the truth? What is the truth? "I just . . . can't."

"She's never asked you to call her Mom?"

I honestly can't remember. Did she? "Maybe," I say finally. Or did I erase the thought from my mind? "Look, Nik, when Tee-tee picked us up at

the orphanage, she told me to call her Tee-tee.
Not Mom. Tee-tee. Besides, she's not our *real*
mom."

Nikky shakes the hammer at me. "She is
too. She's our real *adoptive* mom. Besides, I don't
remember our mom from Russia." He turns
back to the plywood and bashes a headless nail
through with one *whack*. A sob catches in my
throat. I've never seen Nikky so mad at me, and
I hate it.

My inner doll scolds me. Just do it. Say
the word, even if you don't mean it, and make
everyone happy. *Mom.* Such an easy word to roll
off the tongue. Such a hard word to quarry out
of my heart.

Nikky and I lug the plywood sections up
the basement steps and lean them against the
patchwork patio door. "I'll get some wood screws
and the driver."

I tail him as he heads back to the basement.
"And Darya?" He stops halfway down the
steps and looks up at me. The stairwell light
illuminates his hair but shadows his jaw,
narrowing his chubby cheeks, showing me the
outline of the man he'll soon become. "I want
you to call me Nick now, N-I-C-K. Nikky is too
babyish and girly."

"Sure, Nikky," I whisper as he leaps nimbly

from midstep to the basement floor, something a baby could never do.

The mantel clock bongs seven times, and I'm just about to run upstairs to see if Libby wants to watch *Are You Smarter Than A College Professor?* when the doorbell rings.

Tee-tee barrels out of the laundry room aiming a can of pepper spray, and nearly bowls me over. Her face is slick with sweat. "Where's my baby, where's Nikky?" She barely notices me. "Get your brother and go hide." It scares me. Tee-tee has always been my rock, a take-charge person, confident and self-assured. Now she's gibbering.

The bell rings again. I force myself to move. This is silly. Why would Jax politely ring the doorbell? Wouldn't he be more likely to hurl a rock through the window? Jimmy the lock on the garage door?

Tee-tee mouths *Get out* and holds a pinkie and thumb to her cheek, mimicking *Phone Call*. I want to yell, *This is ridiculous*, but my gut warns me to be cautious. We run a shelter after all, and, even though we've remained under the radar over the years, there's a first time for everything. As Tee-tee punches numbers into the kitchen phone, I creep to the front door, staying well to the side in case it *is* Jax, and he decides to

blast it open with his foot—or a shotgun. If only I could see the stoop. But there's no window with a view of the front porch. And no safety chain on the door. The only way to see who's out there is to do what any normal homeowner does when the bell rings. Open the door.

Light flashes at the door windows, three small opaque rectangles imbedded for decoration only, not peeping. Three seconds, then another flash. Light strobes through the living room window, washing the walls in blood red.

*Is he setting fire to our house?*

*Philoxenia's* Rule Number 3 forces me to act: *We are responsible for what happens to our guests, even meeting with danger ourselves rather than involving the women under our protection.*

I wrench the door open. Better to be shot and die instantly than fry.

Bright light blinds me. I shield my face with a hand and squint at a blob of faces before me.

"Are you the deer girl?" a man's voice booms. A microphone is shoved at my mouth. "Are you the youngster who's protesting the town's deer resolution?"

*Great.* I hadn't expected live media coverage.

"What's going on here?" Tee-tee appears by my side, pepper spray aimed. "Who are you

216

people?"

"WSOP-TV. Bill Fleming, anchor." He flips open a notebook. "Filming for News at 11. Your girl's editorial letter was picked up on the 6:00 news, and the station got bombarded with calls from residents. We announced we'd check it out for the late news." He points his pencil at me. "I'd like to talk to this young lady."

Tee-tee steps in front of me. "Anything you want to know, you ask me—"

"It's okay, Tee-tee." I grasp her arm. "I'll speak to them. Outside." I lift my eyes toward the stairway, give a little jerk of the head, hoping Tee-tee will take the clue and go up to hush Libby and Maddie.

I reach into the coat closet for Tee-tee's oversized cable-knit sweater, the one I bought for her last Christmas before I knew how hot the bulky yarn made her. It envelops me like a warm wooly tent. The news guy with the video recorder steps back for a long shot. His harsh bright light torches the front porch and blinds me for a moment. Once again I'm caught in the lights like a flushed deer.

"There she is," someone yells from the yard. "There's the rodent lover." Voices murmur in the darkness, and they sound hard and threatening, not particularly friendly.

When my eyes finally adjust to the dark, I can make out at least fifty people, mostly adults, standing in my yard and driveway. A few hang back along the road lit by a circle of streetlight. All faces are turned toward me, but I can't tell if they're friendly or hostile. Who are these people who've made certain assumptions about me, who came out on a frigid night to confront me because of my beliefs?

One face jumps out at me.

Rawley stands near a parked pickup with a stooped man on crutches, probably his uncle. It's not good, him being here. I can't focus. For some reason I can't think straight when he's around. If I make a fool of myself in front of all these people, I'll be in his line of fire at school, trapped in the spotlight of his unrelenting torment. The thought is a corkscrew to my heart.

Light snow dusts the front steps, so I hold the rail and make my way cautiously down to the sidewalk and slip-slide my way down the slick pavement. I'm not used to walking through a crowd of people, exposed. I feel like a disgraced celebrity who walks through a crush of paparazzi wishing she had a big designer handbag to hide her face.

Two more cars pull up and discharge gawkers. Radio voices squawk as a patrol car

slowly motors by, blue and red lights revolving.

The cops are involved now. This is much worse than I'd ever imagined. I'm upset, as in tears-springing-from-my-eyes upset. In front of people I don't know, about something I really care about. I wish the earth would gape open and swallow me.

I don't have to speak. I could keep my mouth shut. But no, I've been waiting for this moment. "What do you want to know?" I call out, my teeth chattering from cold and, I admit it, fright. "Ask me, and I'll give you a straight answer. I'm only trying to protect creatures that can't defend themselves."

"You tell them, Darya," a woman's voice pipes up. "Some of us are on your side." Camera lights swing in her direction. A jeweled bindi glitters at the center of her forehead.

"We're here for you, Darya," says the boy at her side. Farique, my sweet Moong Dal brainiac. He lifts a hand in greeting. I can breathe now. Someone here is on my side after all. I have a posse.

Rawley's uncle jabs a finger at Farique and his mother. "We don't need you foreign tree-huggers sticking your nose in our business. Deer are pests, and the town's ruling is final."

"Now hold on a bit, Mr. Sandore." Tee-

tee brushes up against my side and circles her arm around me. Her voice is friendly but authoritative, like the one she uses at work. "Nobody's telling you how to run your property. I'm fighting my own battle with these deer. Darya just feels strongly that we don't need to destroy other species, that's all. We should listen to all viewpoints, to be fair."

Tee-tee shocks me with this. But it's a shock that sends a warm certainty sizzling though me. I know that I can completely trust her, that she'd do anything for me, that her motives aren't mixed, and that she only wants what's best for me.

Another voice booms from the dark. "The residents in this town have a legitimate argument to declare the deer population a nuisance. This is America. Voters rule."

Murmurs of approval rise from the crowd.

"Hey," I yell. "This is my property, so let me speak."

Voices die down. I'm left with a silence to fill. It sends me down a rabbit hole of fear.

"In America, the *majority* rules. Not just the voters, but the *majority* of voters." No one speaks out, so I continue. "The town board only passed the resolution based on what they heard from a few members of their constituency, not the town

as a whole."

Tee-tee squeezes my shoulder. She gives me a little celebratory shake, then clears her throat and backs me up. "Seems like what Darya means is that a few squeaky wheels got the grease."

The crowd is clearly divided. *Yeahs* and *nahs* merge and clash. I suppose what's driving them crazy is that I'm taking this deer issue and using it in a way they don't like. Some must feel I'm downright evil, because I'm upsetting their culling plan when they thought it was a done deal. If I look at it that way, I can almost understand what they're doing. But I don't understand. What I really want to do is pound their heads with a hammer.

Bill Fleming cuts in and addresses the camera, reporting like a war correspondent. "Folks, this is the issue that's tearing apart the town of Twin Lakes. The bitter dispute between those who want to save the deer and those who want to destroy them. Live from the Morningside subdivision. Now back to you."

The camera lights fade, and Tee-tee pulls Fleming aside. I seem to have become invisible. A few people break from the group and head for their cars, stamping their feet for warmth.

Rawley helps his uncle into the pickup and slams the passenger door shut. He notices me

staring at him and walks toward me. "I've been thinking about what you said, Russky." He turns up his collar against the cold. His coat is stained and shapeless, probably another cast-off of his uncle's. "I'm not totally against your stand, you know."

"You're not? Can you get your uncle to post his land again?"

He shrugs. "Probably not. Me and my uncle don't always see eye to eye. We're both stubborn. I can't make him do anything once he gets his mind set."

"So nothing's going to change?"

"Probably not—unless my parents come back and try to make him see differently."

"Your parents? You mean your mom too? She isn't . . ."

"Isn't what?"

I hate to say the word, but there's no way around it. "Dead?"

Rawley jerks his head back. "God, no. She's okay. The transplant went fine." He smiles as he says that, but his voice trembles.

"Oh, that's good! You know the gossipers around here, they just can't keep anything straight." I'm babbling, I know it.

"She was close to dying. She needed a new kidney and one was available in Boston. She and

my dad flew there, so I came here to stay with my uncle and keep up with school." He shivers as cold gusts over us. "It's hard to get used to, this weather." He jerks his head toward the truck. "And him."

*Stranger in a strange land.* Just like me. "I so understand. Believe me."

"How could you? You've got your family here, your mom. You live here."

I'm in no mood for explaining, so I change the subject. "What could your parents do to make your uncle see differently?"

"My parents are like you, in a way. They own a dive shop in St. Thomas, and they're always instructing tourist divers to leave the sea life alone instead of collecting specimens for souvenirs."

"They believe in protecting sea life?"

"Protecting? I guess you could call it that. It's more like letting things be."

"And I believe in letting deer be. It's as simple as that."

"Hah! No, Russky, it's not simple at all. Take a look around." He arcs his arm toward the remaining mob. "Some folks here are ready to take you down."

I look away for a moment to gauge the crowd's mood. They stand in small groups, camps

for and against, as Bill Fleming moves among them taking notes. The sneering ones probably want to burn me at the stake, or boil me in oil, or brand a scarlet letter on my forehead. I feel a leaden lump in my gut. Everything I do seems to turn out wrong, even when I try to do what I think is right. The camera light sweeps away from the crowd and swings toward me.

I feel a tug on my sweater. A child's head bobs at my waist.

"Maddie! What are you doing here?" I scoop her up and bundle her within my sweater. This is major bad news. She's been seen by all, even the home viewing audience. If Jax is here somewhere. . .

My eyes scan the crowd. But the crowd isn't looking at us. Instead, they're focused on something in my backyard, near the tree line.

Maddie's head pokes through the top of my sweater. She points a finger. "Rudolph!"

A shadowy herd of deer stands motionless, cautiously watching us watching them. Their ears are pricked forward as if listening for danger.

"They're so pretty," someone says in a hushed voice.

"Pretty good targets is more like it," a harsh voice barks. "Let's get a few of 'em. We'll have a

freezer full of venison this year."

A few of his buddies give a cheer, then clap each other on the back.

"Not on our property, you don't." I snug my sweater tighter around Maddie. "Go home, all of you!" In the background Libby's voice calls out for Maddie, from the house. This is crazy. I have to get Maddie inside, away from the crowds and lights.

*Clang-clang-clang.*

Nikky's on the front steps with his pot and spoon, banging on his homemade deer repellent.

The buck gives a shrill snort and cuts the earth with his front hoofs in a resounding thump. The skittish herd prances backward a few steps, ready to bound off.

"Scram, deer," Nikky yells. "Or you'll be dead meat."

The buck turns and plunges headlong into the darkness. The does bound after him, tails flashing white.

"B-b-baby's hurt." Maddie shivers against me.

A lone fawn limps after the herd. Its left front leg is cocked at an angle, and he holds it high off the ground as he wobbles across the snow and into the dark.

"That one will be dead before morning," the deep voice snarls. "Most likely got hit by a car."

Tomorrow. How quickly the line between life and death is crossed.

He motions to his buddies. "I got my shotgun in the truck. I can take it down quick before it suffers too much."

A scream builds up inside me. My mouth is so cold I can barely get the words out. "Everyone off my property." I stagger forward with my bundle. Maddie whimpers under my sweater. If my hands were free, I'd be pounding their ugly faces. But I need to switch tactics and try for pity. "Don't you people care? It's just a helpless deer. If your dog or cat was injured, wouldn't you do everything to try to save it?"

Rawley's uncle leans out the truck window. "Perfect example right here, folks. We got too many rodents in this town, and they're getting maimed. Let's do away with the bunch of them."

I can't handle this with Maddie so exposed. A glance at the house tells me Tee-tee's busy shooing Libby back inside, keeping her out of sight and calming her down. I catch Farique's attention and beckon him over.

"Unzip your coat."

He glances back at his mother, then follows

my order without question or complaint. I slide Maddie out of my sweater-cocoon and bundle her into the warmth of Farique's parka. "Take her back to the house, promise? I have to save the deer."

Rawley comes up behind me and grips my arm. "Hold up, Russky. Face the facts. Nothing can save that deer now. You have to let things be."

I yank away from him. I want to scream, bite, pummel him with my fists.

I can't—won't—accept what he says. I'll capture the deer and take it to the vet's. I'll nurse it myself and make it part of our family, our new pet. I'll adopt it.

A moan rises in my throat, so I gulp cold air to tamp it down. My nose bubbles, my eyes water. My entire system is bracing for a meltdown.

I run at a man wearing a hunter's tag and pound on his back as he reaches inside the cab for his shotgun. We're caught in a spotlight as the news camera films.

He turns with an arm up, laughing and cursing. "C'mon little girl, we're just having some fun here."

I shove him backward and he slips, knocking his head against the doorframe. "Goddamn you, girl."

This is so totally unlike me. This ferocity welling up inside me terrifies me. My whole belief system got flushed down the tubes with one shove. I've never meant to harm anyone or anything and here in this flash of rage, I've done just that. I've physically hurt someone, and I could cringe with shame. It goes against my values. It goes against who I am. I'm no better than a deer slayer. Or a wife beater.

He comes at me with hands stretched open, his big thumbs ready to crush my throat. I wheel backwards, slip in the snow, and hit the ground hard. The camera zooms in for a close-up, and the light blinds me. With an arm shielding my face, I struggle to my feet and lurch toward the hunter. To do what, I don't know. Just to stop him somehow.

Rawley steps between us. "Come hunt on my uncle's land," he says in his smooth rhythmic voice. "You'd be doing us a real favor . . ." His voice trails off as they move away.

I curl into fetal position and whimper with fear. I don't know what to do. I am all the deer have, and I can't think of the first thing to do.

Rawley's boots fill my sight. His hands are on my shoulders, lifting me up to face him. "Keep cool, Russky. My uncle says you can't fight city hall. Whatever that means."

"I *can* fight city hall. But I can't keep cool."

"Big surprise. But from now on you will be. Just stand next to me and be quiet. And don't try to hit anyone, because it won't help your cause."

My *cause.* I hadn't thought of it that way but it has a nice ring to it. Darya's Cause. That's Rawley's power—that he can smile at me and make me start thinking whatever he wants.

*With a bawl of pain, the fawn limps through the leafless brush following the herd's scent. Caution and fear shoot through him.*

*But also joy. He saw her, the young human. He stops and turns, pricking his ears in her direction. Yes, he can still hear her. She mewls and yelps the way he did when glaring lights shot out from around a curve and blinded him as he crossed the road. Terrified, he stopped for an instant, quivering in fright. Something hard and cold shot past him, then hit his rear quarters as he leapt away. The force picked him up and*

tossed him to one side. His front legs crumpled under him. But he scrambled to his feet and bounded away through the woods in terror.

She is weeping for him.

The pain in his leg lessens. He whirls and leaps through the darkness.

# Strangers in the Dark

*Maddie?*
*Where's Maddie?*

It's just hit me she's gone. What did I do with her? I've lost her.

No . . . I remember now. I handed her off to Farique because I absolutely trust him. We've been classmates since kindergarten, and it doesn't hurt that he has a crush on me and wants to please me. In all the media frenzy—the TV interview and everyone storming at me—I totally forgot about Maddie. Some fine mother I'd make who'd dump her kid on a bystander and walk off, lost in her need for self-preservation.

Tee-tee waves at me from the porch. No sign of Farique and Maddie, so he must have hustled her inside the way I asked. I like a guy I can count on, one with intelligence and reliability. A guy who doesn't smart-mouth me, or make me his target. A guy who supports me and doesn't care who I am or where I came from. A guy like Farique.

I only wish he were someone else.

Rawley doesn't treat me with half the respect Farique shows me, so why am I attracted to him? I thought I had a good feel for the different types of guys out there until Rawley appeared on the menu. Libby isn't the only one who needs a swift kick in the knickers. I'm next in line.

I cup my hands and call to Rawley over the raised quarreling voices, the newscaster, the squad car squawks. "Rawley, wait up."

My clogs are slushed over, every step a *squish-squish*. I snug the sweater tighter and tuck the collar under my chin. My anger heated me up, but it's dissipated, and the shirt against my skin feels clammy, sticky. A hot flash of my own making.

I'm puffing clouds of white vapor by the time I reach him. "Have you seen Farique and the little girl, Maddie?"

"Farique had to carry his mom to a squad car." He slides his uncle's crutches into the truck bed. "Her water broke. They left for the

232

hospital."

"She's pregnant?" This is mind-blowing news. I didn't notice her baby bump under her dark, oversized coat. His mother wasn't that old, at least not as old as Tee-tee, but after a sixteen-year gap I'm surprised she's still in the baby-making business.

"I told him I'd make sure the little girl was safe."

"You took Maddie inside?"

"I sent her off to your Tee-tee Mom when you went on your rant. I couldn't very well use her for a shield, do you think?"

"Not a good idea." Relief whooshes through me. Maddie's safe.

"Your little sister looks a lot like you. She's a real cutie."

*He thinks I'm cute.* "Oh, she's not my sister. She's only staying with us for a while."

He slams the gate and moves to the driver's side door. "Did you really think you'd beat that guy up? He was only yanking your chain, Russky. Putting on a show for his buddies and trying to rile you."

"Sure, he's doing that *now*. But you saw his gun. He's a hunter. He's seen the herd. He'll be back with his buddies, jacking the deer on our property. I know *that* for a fact."

Rawley pulls keys from his pocket and jingles them in his hand. "Maybe not. He knows he's been caught on camera. He'll probably be pretty embarrassed when it airs on the late news, especially after being attacked by a girl half his size."

The passenger side window slides down. "Stay clear of her, boy," his uncle's voice rasps from inside the cab. "She's a troublemaker."

*And you're a stubborn old coot.* I bite my tongue, fighting the urge to taunt a disabled old man. The news guy would be all over it. I don't need a reputation for beating up on hunters *and* senior citizens.

Rawley slides into the driver's seat and tucks a blanket around his uncle's legs. He beckons me over and hangs his head out the window. "The heater's kaput." Then, in a low voice, "My uncle's really a fair guy, once he's heard all sides. It's this accident that's got him cranky. I think he needs help." Rawley whirls his finger in a circle at his head.

"Maybe Tee-tee can recommend a counselor," I tell him quietly. "That's a service of her Helpline agency."

"Thanks, and ask her about a nursing aide. Uncle hasn't showered since the accident. Or changed his underwear as far as I can tell."

*Mr. Poopypants.*

"I've threatened to run him through a car wash. Without a car."

"Maybe Tee-tee should stop over sometime." *Me too.* "In a professional capacity." *So I can see you alone.* "To assess his needs."

"Sounds great, but ask her to call me first," he cocks his head toward his uncle, "so I can prepare the old guy." Rawley settles back on the driver's seat and starts the engine. He turns his face toward me again. "And maybe you can come with her."

This invitation is the best news on the worst day of my existence.

"You've got a real knack for speaking out and bossing folks around. We could use some of that around our place." He gives me a two-fingered salute as he drives off.

I'm not sure whether to take it as a compliment or a criticism, but I'm not wasting any time worrying about it. What's foremost in my mind is how cool and casual he maneuvers around the parked squad cars as he breaks the law, underage and driving at night, while I'm still on training wheels.

I stomp my clogs on the porch mat and push through the front door. A high whining noise

comes from upstairs. My first thought is that our cat is trapped in the laundry chute, but then I realize it's Libby.

My wet clogs slip on the tile. The floorboards squeak as Libby goes from room to room. "What's going on, Libby?" I call up the stairwell. I'm afraid she's having a breakdown. "What's wrong?"

She appears at the landing, wild-eyed and panting. Ethan is squirming on her shoulder. Her voice comes out in a high-pitched whine. "I can't find Maddie." She turns abruptly and her voice echoes down the hall. "Maddie. Maddie, where are you? Tell Mommy where you're hiding. No more games. Come out right now."

"Tee-tee's got her. She's okay, Libby."

Libby comes into view again, and heaves a shuddery breath. I sign a thumbs-up, and she gives me a nod and a weak smile. Ethan starts fretting, so she bouncy-walks him back to her bedroom.

My reflection in the entry mirror startles me. My face is chapped red, and my hair's a frizzed mess. My bones ache from the cold. I kick off my clogs, peel off my soaked socks, and shuck off my sweater. I unsnap my wet jeans and let them drop to the floor. I don't care who sees me. News at 11: Naked Russian Girl Bares All.

The fireplace doors are open, with newspaper

crumpled under the grate. I make a dash for the oversized comfy armchair, sink into its warmth, and spread an afghan over my legs.

Footsteps pound down the stairs. Libby swoops around the corner, holding Ethan face forward on her hip. She stands before me, jiggling him in a soothing up-down rhythm. "She's still with Tee-tee, right?"

"Don't worry about anything that happened tonight, Lib. I caught Maddie before anyone could get a good look at her and wrapped her in my sweater. I had to hand her over to a friend of mine, but he made sure Maddie got to Tee-tee all safe and sound."

"Who got to me all safe and sound?" Tee-tee stands in the doorway with an armful of split wood.

My eyes dart past Tee-tee to the empty space behind her.

"You don't have Maddie?" I already know the answer.

I leap out of my chair. *Maddie. Gone.* I fly past Tee-tee to the mudroom.

"I'll come with you." Tee-tee drops the kindling on the hearth. "You can't go out there alone."

I throw on my parka. Pants. I need pants. "Yes I can." I'm absolutely positive about this.

"I've created this whole mess myself. It's my fault there's a media stakeout. If I hadn't stirred things up with my deer . . ." The truth sticks in my throat. ". . . with my deer *obsession*, Maddie would be safe. We'd all be safe."

"I forbid you to go out, Darya." Tee-tee moves to block the door. She stands like a prison guard, face stern, arms crossed on her chest. "It's too dangerous. I'm your mother, and I absolutely forbid it."

I whirl on her and blurt, "You're not my mother."

Tee-tee's face crumples. I should throw my arms around her and tell her I love her, but my heart feels like a small hard nut, uncrackable.

"You have to stay here with Nikky and Libby. They need you." Tee-tee's baggy snow pants hang by the door, and I wrestle my way into them. I stab my bare feet into boots.

"And I need you, sweetie. If anything ever happened to you, I'd die. I'd honestly die. You and Nikky are my life."

Guilt sweeps over me. Why am I so hard on this woman who's always been there for us? For *me*? "I'll be fine, Tee-tee, really. I know how the deer jackers operate. I know our property like I know my own name. I'll just make a big circle and come right back. Maddie's only two. She

can't have gotten that far. She's probably taken off after that baby deer, the one with the broken leg."

Tee-tee hesitates, then drops her arms to her sides. She gnaws her lower lip, something she does when she's undecided.

"Look, give me your pepper spray. Besides, Maddie might come back on her own. You'll need to be here, because Libby's a basket case."

"I'm calling the police," she says, heading for the kitchen phone. "Jax might have been in that crowd. He might have taken her."

While Tee-tee reports into the phone, I flick on all the outdoor lights, then step outside. The lights are hardly necessary. A full moon, a silvery luminescent wafer, bathes the backyard.

A White Night, illuminated by the moon, not the sun.

Tee-tee might be right. Jax may have Maddie. If he was the anonymous caller who knew the code word, he also knows our address. He might have been in the crowd, watching, and spotted Maddie as she raced across the yard to me. He would have seen me hand Maddie to Farique, then watched Farique shift her to Rawley, and later spotted the send off to Tee-tee. Jax might have intercepted her at that point, although I can't imagine how. Unless somewhere in the mix

she was unsupervised and open to abduction.

Or maybe Maddie was simply drawn to the hobbling deer, wanting to befriend Rudolph.

Either way, Maddie is lost.

Stepping across the yard I head for the tree line, the spot where the wounded fawn followed his herd into the woods. I figure Maddie is close by, within yards of the house. At two, she can't get far, not in the dark and with the snow cover.

Unless Jax has her. But if that's so, he won't leave without Libby and Ethan.

Pine limbs hang like shadows overhead. A sudden wind bends the pine tops and bits of snow sift down on my head. In my rush I forgot a hat, and now my ears tingle with cold.

Something darts across my path. It scurries into the brush, dragging a fat tail. Red eyes glow and blink, then disappear.

A high-pitched cry rings from the oak grove to my left.

"Maddie?" I listen for a reply, but there's only the soft rush of traffic out on the interstate. Then a quick rustle of dry leaves under the pines. I chant to keep myself sane, focused. *Squirrels, chipmunks, squirrels, chipmunks.*

I've been in these woods more times than I can count, but this path seems unfamiliar, sloping down and away from the back road. I push

through a clump of leafless brush—leafless, but not without thorns that snag my nylon parka. A cloud passes over the moon and pitches me into blackness. I could smack myself for trekking out here without a flashlight. Where the hell am I?

My footing gives way, and, before I can catch my balance, I'm sliding down an embankment toward a gurgling sound. My knees and feet sink into the slush of a small stream. The cold seeps into my boots, and my toes go stiff.

Again I hear a child's cry, close by, off to my right this time.

"Maddie?" I want to scream it, but know I need to keep my voice low, controlled. "Is that you, baby?"

Ice crunches, then the swoosh-crush of something big, something moving slowly through the dry brush. The woods are awash in moonlight, but I can't see any movement, only hear the approach.

Louder this time. "Maddie?" My voice sounds braver than it is. "No more hide-and-seek. Mommy's waiting."

Silence.

"Tee-tee's got treats. A juice box. You can stab the straw in."

Something huge. Something near.

*Get out of here.*

I run, flailing through the pine boughs. I stumble over an exposed tree root and put my hands out to stop my fall. My palms scrape against rough bark. Over my own whimpering is the *huff huff* of labored panting behind me, close, much too close.

I drop to all fours and put my back to a tree trunk. I'm winded, my throat raw and burning. I'm wet with sweat inside my parka. I unzip it and let the icy air wash over my chest. A lump in my pocket bumps against my hip. *Pepper spray.* I wrest the tube out and fumble at the tab with stiff, cold fingers.

Arms grasp me from behind and lift me off my feet. A hand claps over my mouth.

"Shhh," a voice hisses in my ear.

I dig the fingers of both my hands into the hand covering my mouth, but the wrist and arm holding me are taut and muscled. I can't budge it.

A whimper rises in my throat. I swing my fists backwards, but he wraps his arm tighter around my chest and pins my arms. I'm wedged in a vise, holding my breath and counting the racing beats of my heart.

His voice rasps low in my ear. "No screaming, okay?"

Wheezing, I give a quick nod. One finger

slips from my mouth. Then two.

When my teeth are clear, I bite his hand.

"Shit!" He claps his hand back over my mouth, crushing my jaw with steely fingers.

I lash out with my free fist, punching it hard as I can at the shadowy face behind me. I stomp on his foot, kick backward at his shins.

He knees me hard in the butt, then grunts in my ear. "Cut it out, Russky."

I go limp just long enough for him to let loose. I swivel around in a fury. "What are *you* doing out here? Isn't it past your bedtime?"

Rawley shakes me. "Quiet," he croaks. "You trying to get yourself killed?"

"Maddie's out here," I say, dropping my voice to a whisper. "You bailed." I pound my fists on his chest. "You told me you gave Maddie to Tee-tee."

Rawley shivers and shoves his hands in his pockets. "We got our signals mixed, I guess." He looks down, stomps snow off his boots. "I thought your mom saw me wave. I sent the little one running in her direction."

"Maddie's only two. You have to take her by the hand and lead her." *Guys.* Some are clueless when it comes to kids.

"Yeah . . . sorry." His breath comes in white puffs. "When I got home, Farique called me from

the hospital."

"Farique?" I'm stunned by this unexpected twist.

"He was worried about Maddie, so he called your mom first. She filled him in."

"And then he called you?" This is so unlikely that it takes me a moment to process. "Why *you* of all people?"

"Why *not* me?" Anger edges his voice. "You don't get it, do you? Not all guys are rivals when it comes to liking the same girl. Farique wants to help you. *I* want to help you. And I've got wheels. A lost kid is more important than a bruised male ego. Wise up, Russky."

"Oh." I'm not sure which surprises me most, the fact that I have two suitors who aren't rivals for my affection or that Rawley is so articulate when he's fired up.

"So that's why I'm here. To help you find Maddie."

"I don't *need* your help. I can find her my—"

A crunch of snow startles me. I turn to see a man standing not twenty feet away. A man out for an unlikely stroll through the woods. A man holding Maddie bundled into his varsity hockey jacket. Her arms cling to his neck.

"Hey, Maddie," I call quietly to her. "We've been looking for you. Mommy's been looking for

you."

Maddie tightens her grip on her father's neck and pushes her face into his collar. "Daddy?"

"Hey, mon, you found her." Rawley slips into his easy island patter. "We've been looking all over for this little one." He steps forward and holds out his arms. "We'll take her back to her mommy now."

Jax tightens his grip on Maddie. "Thanks, but I'm her father. She's safe now." He gives Maddie a quick bounce. "Aren't you, honey? Everything's cool."

"But her mommy's worried." I can't let him just walk off with Maddie.

Maddie's head jerks up. "Mommy?"

Jax strokes her hair. "Let's go get Mommy, sweetheart." He starts in the direction of our house.

"She doesn't want you." My voice echoes through the quiet woods. "Leave Libby alone."

Jax strides up to me, defiant. The odor of beer and cigarettes clings to him like an aura. "Get her out here," he growls, getting in my face. His eyes bulge with rage, and his breath is hot. "Get Libby. I know she's in there. Tell her she can't have Maddie unless she comes out."

"Forget it." I resist the urge to grab a handful of his jacket and yank him off-balance. I need

to handle this without riling him up. I've seen firsthand how he settles arguments with his fists. I tamp down my temper and sort through options. How would Tee-tee handle this? What if I say the wrong thing? I plunge ahead with some daddy ego-stroking. "You're so good with Maddie. Look, I know you really care about your kids and want to do what's best for them."

Jax practically snarls at me. "I don't care what you know or what you think I should do. I'll settle this with Libby. Get her. *Now*."

I spit the words out. "You'll settle it all right. In court."

He curses and slices his free hand at my head. I fall backward, land hard. His foot kicks at my ribs, but I scuttle sideways.

Maddie shrieks, and Jax hitches her higher over his shoulder.

With a roar Rawley launches across the open space and swings a fist, but he's no match for a brawny six-foot athlete. Jax swings out with a roundhouse punch and slugs Rawley's jaw with such ferocity that he flies back a few yards and lands with a thud on the hard-packed snow.

"Leave him alone." I scan the ground for a rock, a tree limb, anything to use as a weapon.

"Leave him alone," Jax mimics in a high girly voice, then says with a sneer, "Leave *me* and my

*family* alone."

I drop to my knees beside Rawley and cradle his head in my hands, holding the bones of his skull. Rawley's eyes are rolled up in his head, and his mouth gapes. "Rawley." My ragged breath puffs white. "Can you hear me?" I place two fingers on his throat searching for a pulse, but my icicle fingers have lost sensation.

Jax coolly observes me. He shushes Maddie, loudly, harsher this time. No longer the kind, concerned father.

"Libby," he bellows in the direction of the house. "Libby, goddamn it, get your ass out here, bitch. And bring my son."

Maddie hiccups baby sobs and beats her tiny hands against her father's shoulder. She wriggles to get down and away from him. Jax tightens his grip on her. "Damn it, Maddie. Quit it before I belt you one."

That does it. I'm taking Maddie before he makes good on his threat. Better he slug me than her. I shuck off my parka and ball it into a pillow to support Rawley's head. I'm ready to spring, a cheetah out for the kill to protect her baby.

Ice-laden pine boughs tinkle and click, quivering in a quick wind gust. A shadowy form steps quietly out of the moonlit woods. Its thick chest and broad back move with a powerful

leonine grace. The buck snorts, flanks quivering, and strides stiff-legged toward Jax.

"What the hell?" Jax's cocky attitude turns to fear. He shrinks back, his face a mix of disbelief and horror.

The buck bares his teeth, his head thrown back so far the antlers rest on his back. He paws the earth, whistles through his distended nares.

"Tyransores Rex," Maddie yells.

Jax gives the house a quick glance as if gauging the distance he'll need to cover, running with a toddler in his arms. He slowly lowers Maddie to the ground and gives her a little shove toward me. "Go to the nice girl, Maddie."

The buck steps forward and stops, tensing his rear quarters and snorting. He scents the air, then shakes his rack. Ears twitching, he waits, as if for a signal.

Jax squats and picks up an exposed rock. He chucks it hard, whacking the buck in the flanks. "Get," he bellows. "Get outta here."

The buck slashes the ground, ready to charge, gouts of snow spraying the air behind its haunches. He lowers his head, extends his forks, and fakes a charge at Jax.

Jax plunges across the yard toward the house. The crusted snow slows him down, each step a slow-motion effort of plucking out a foot

before putting it down again. He stumbles, falls to one knee, then rises again, supporting himself with one hand on the ground and the other arm stretched out for balance, leaving his chest an easy target.

The buck crouches, forks thrust forward and charges, this time for real. I scoop up Maddie and hug her to me, holding her head against my shoulder, her face buried in my hair. I can't allow her to see her father hurt. She's seen enough hurt in her two years.

An antler point pierces Jax's shoulder. His mouth opens as if to scream, although no sound comes. He tumbles backward, a patch of red staining his jacket and another dark stain blooming at the crotch of his jeans. He's wet himself like a two year old.

Jax crumples to the snow with a moan. His head is thrown back, his words high and pleading. "Call the bugger off."

As if I had any control over a wild animal bent on killing. Maddie whimpers against me, her small shoulders shivering with cold and fright. Sure, I want Jax punished for what he did to Libby. He deserves to be bashed and gored in the same way he abused his wife and messed up his family.

The buck chops his forehooves, then wheels

and lunges in a single bound.

A scream rings out, echoing up my spine and ending with a shiver in my scalp. Jax squeals like a rabbit in a wolf's jaws. He blubbers, pleading for his life. It's pitiful, and I can't bear it any longer.

"*Stoy*," I command, the Russian word leaping to my mouth. "Stop. You're killing him."

The buck turns and shakes his crest at me, defiant, as if saying *no*. His ears shoot backward, then forward, as if processing my words. He stands motionless for a moment, fire in his eyes and the black ridge of his back bristling.

He steps forward and sniffs at Jax.

Jax whimpers and draws himself into a ball. He throws up his arms to cover his head.

The buck prods Jax with his nose.

"No," I order again, my arm raised. I will not be defied.

The buck takes a few steps toward me, his head cocked. Our eyes lock. With a whistling snort he rears and wheels, then charges into the underbrush.

"Daddy," Maddie bawls with body-shuddering sobs. "Daddy's hurt."

"It's okay, baby," I say, rocking her. I kneel by Rawley and place my hand on him. His chest moves up and down as he lies unconscious. Still breathing, alive.

A voice calls my name. A circle of light bobs and flashes through the trees.

"Tee-tee," I yell back. "Tee-tee, here."

Her voice grows fainter. The light arcs away to the left. She's going in the wrong direction. "This way, Tee-tee," I scream.

"Tee-tee, here." Why can't she hear me? Why can't she find me? I need help. I need her warmth, her blast-furnace heat. I need the woman who has been a mother to me for these ten years.

The cry that I had been fighting back for so many years escapes me in a groan of grief and loneliness. "MOM," I howl from the depths of my soul. "MOMMY!"

# Mother Russia, Grandfather Lenin

Heavy tasseled curtains frame a dark wooden stage. The enormous cut-glass chandelier overhead dims and tinkles as Tchaikovsky's symphony thrums through the auditorium. I press my chin atop the gilded railing of our box in the Mariinsky Theatre, my dress bunched between my legs. The student ballet troupe leaps and pirouettes toward center stage, fairy creatures trailing delicate wispy wings.

I reach behind me and tug at my mother's silky gown. *"Krasivaya, Mam."*

Mama shushes me, patting the seat between her and my father. As I bounce into the seat, my shoe buckle snags on the gauzy hem of my dress, my best holiday dress, the one Mama fashioned from her own tutu. Mama shoots me a stern look, but Papa winks. He turns his head toward the aisle and lifts a hand to his mouth. His jaws flex open in a huge yawn. Ballet bores him. He much prefers the Moscow Circus—*moskovskiy tsirk*—and the Circus on Ice—*tsirk na l'du*—with its ice-skating bears.

Mama frees my buckle, then bends to whisper in my ear. Waves of lavender rise from the dark *U* in her scoop-necked bodice. "Yes, the dancers are very beautiful, but they train very hard. Perhaps you will be one someday."

I thrill at the thought. Me, a ballerina. Flying over the stage.

Mama couldn't have guessed then what would become of her dreams of a daughter being accepted into the Academy of Ballet. She didn't aim quite far—or high—enough. With a leap into the future, I'd be flying over the Atlantic Ocean instead of the theater stage. More of a caged circus bear than an ethereal sugarplum fairy.

After the performance Papa holds open the small wooden door to our box, allowing Mama and me to pass through first. He follows behind, ducking his head so as not to bonk it on the low archway. I wasn't aware at the time, but thinking

back I'm reminded of a child's playhouse.

We move with the crowd toward the exit doors. I yawn and rub my eyes. It is hours past my bedtime. Papa lifts me into his arms, and I rest my head on his shoulder. Humid summer air washes over me as we step out onto the blinding sidewalk, which reflects the slanting golden rays of a White Nights sun.

Mama and Papa stop to chat with friends. I peek over Papa's shoulder and squint into the sun. A group of tourists poses for photos in front of the theater. They are so unlike us in their thick-soled white sneakers and designer jeans. They bray like donkeys when they laugh, their wide smiling mouths revealing dazzling, straight white teeth. I don't like these Ameriki strangers. Little did I realize I'd soon become one of them.

A group of boys approaches the tourists. A pack of stray dogs—at least a dozen—patters down the street behind them. "Gum. Gum, please," the boys beg with hands out.

The tourists pat their pockets and reach into purses. Most shake their heads and shrug, palms up in a sorry gesture. But one teen girl in a university T-shirt fishes around in her backpack and pulls out a cellophane packet. The boys close in on her. She dispenses the white rectangles inside.

254

"*Spasibo*," each boy says, taking the gum, then handing the girl a small shiny object. "Peace and friendship. Peace and friendship."

"Papa," I whisper into his ear. I jab a finger at the gum beggars. "What's that? What are those boys giving the girl?"

Papa turns and follows my finger. "Pins," he tells me. "Pins glorifying Mother Russia and our Grandfather Lenin."

"But why? The gum is free."

Papa sniffs. "Russian people are not beggars. We always give something in return."

How different America is. Tee-tee gets calls from needy people all the time, and she directs them to food pantries and shelters and clinics—all free. But they give nothing in return. Sometimes not even a thank you.

Philoxenia's Rule Number 5: *Nothing is expected in return for our services.*

I guess I should tell Tee-tee what a good person she is. And thank her. *Spasibo.*

# Just Call Me Mom

No school today. A sleet storm moved through late last night, just after the ambulance hauled Jax away to the hospital. Storm or no storm, I wouldn't have gone. I'm shaky and have a bruise on my hip the size of a softball.

From the kitchen I look out over our sun-sparkled yard. Light flurries dot the air, blowing up, down, sideways. The low sun sends golden beams through the window. On the sill a dark green ivy, rooted in one of Nikky's old baby bottles, grows toward the window, catching rays.

A brownish-gray dot moves in the distance. Black eyes. The white slash of a tail. A lone doe.

Without taking my eyes off the doe, I reach for an apple in the fruit bowl. I move quickly through the mudroom, toe into clogs, and quietly unlatch the door.

The orange sun hangs just above the tree line, sending slanting rays toward me. My feet make *shishing* sounds as I tread through the new, fine snow toward the doe. Sensing me, but unafraid, she grazes on the exposed greenery. Every so often she raises her head and pricks her ears forward.

"Hey, girl."

At the sound of my voice, the doe raises her head and pauses, rigid, staring at me. Her large ears are set forward. A tangle of vegetation hangs from her mouth as she ceases feeding.

I take a few steps toward her, crooning as I would to baby Ethan. She catches my scent, shivers, and steps back.

I hold out the apple on the palm of my hand. "Here's a treat for you, lady. Come eat."

*The Dar-Ya speaks to me and offers food. I must accept or risk offending her. I will be brave. She will not harm me. She is my sister.*

The doe does not wait for me to come to her. She steps forward and sniffs the apple, her nostrils flaring as she studies the scent. She

stretches her neck toward me and takes the apple with her black lips. Her mouth is soft as a glove and warm as it brushes my hand. She crunches the apple in a single bite, then tosses her head. Apple juice sprays over me.

*The Dar-Ya opens her mouth and makes happy noises like the morning birds. Her scent is as sweet as the fruit she has given me. If I offer my head, will she give me her blessing?*

She's close enough to touch, but I don't try to pet her like I would a domesticated cat or dog. I might scare her away.

*Why does she not touch me? Have I offended her?*

I wish I'd brought two apples. I didn't realize she'd be so hungry or so tame. "Go now," I tell her, waving her away. "Go join your herd."

*Oh, she tires of me. But I must ask one last favor, her healing blessing on my little one who cannot keep up with his brothers and sisters. Come to me, little one.*

*Dry leaves crackle and pop as the frail fawn limps out of the woods. His broken leg is cocked at an angle, but he makes his way toward his mother on three legs.*

"You're still alive." I'm so happy I could nearly squeal and break out in a jig. The doe nudges him toward me. He half-hitches over and

takes a tentative sniff at my jeans. I can't help myself. I must touch him, although I know it breaks all the rules. My fingertips run over his silky nut-brown fur. I slide a hand lightly down his hurt leg. He watches me with one dark eye but doesn't flinch.

*Heal him, O Dar-Ya. Your sister begs you to heal her baby. I will be forever in your debt.*
A *boom* sounds in the distance. Hunters.
*The bad sound. Little one, we must go.*

With two springs she bounds away from me, then stops, waiting for her baby to catch up. He hobbles lightly, as though he's grown accustomed to moving on only three legs. Together they leap away through the trees.

"Run, lady, run," I call after her. "Don't let them get you." Empty-handed, I turn back to the house.

Mom—how strange the word is—waits for me at the back door. She isn't smiling. "You were feeding the deer again, weren't you, Darya." It's not a question.

I kick at the snow with the toe of my clog. "Yes. But I have to. I can't let them starve. No one else seems to care."

Mom looks at me as if maybe all the media attention has affected my IQ. "Do you really love these deer so much that you'd give your life to helping them?"

I think about it for a moment. "Yes, I do. I can't explain it, but I really do."

"I can understand that. I guess I'm like that too. Otherwise I wouldn't do what I do for a living."

"Helping strangers."

"Helping strangers. Establishing Philoxenia House. Running the Helpline. You and I are incredibly alike. I swear the gods were smiling

upon me the day you came into my life."

Smiling because they were playing a practical joke on her?

"But you really didn't want me. Just Nikky, right?"

Mom huffs, both surprised and angry. Her face glows a steamy hot-flash red. "Of course I wanted you. Whatever made you think I didn't?"

"You said you went to Russia to adopt one child—a baby." I try to keep from yelling. "But you had to take me too."

"I didn't *have* to take you. I *wanted* to take you. No, you weren't adorable in the usual sense. You were sullen, scrawny, your hair full of snarls. I didn't want an older child, it's true. I had come to adopt a baby. But I could see you loved Nikky. You didn't want him to leave. At that moment, that very instant, you were a child of my own heart, someone who cared about others. Separation never entered my mind." Mom shuts her eyes, silent for a moment, remembering. "You and Nikky were obviously a family. *I* was the outsider."

I hear the truth in her voice. I need to know more. "Why did you come for us when you were so old? Did you make a mistake not having children of your own?"

Mom's eyes are watery, from the cold or the truth, I can't tell. "I thought taking care of strangers would fill my life. It did for a while. I immersed myself in *philoxenia*, the ancient sacred relationship between guest and host." She reaches out to a low-hanging branch and runs her fingers down it, stripping off the dried brown leaves. "After a while, I felt empty, as bare and empty as this tree. I was always giving, never taking anything for myself. I had no one, no family. I was alone, a stranger in this world, taking care of other strangers."

*Tee-tee, a stranger?* We *are* alike, more than I could have ever guessed.

"I always felt like a stranger too," I confess. "Because we're not related."

Mom puts her arm around me. "Sweetie, we're all strangers on this planet. All of a sudden we appear, through no doing of our own. Our parents meet by chance, and one particular sperm beats out a million others to join with one particular egg. Off by a second, and we'd be different people entirely. How strange is that?"

"I know. I thought the same thing about Libby, how one tiny decision changed her life. That maybe if she hadn't been so hot on Jax in high school, she'd be in med school now."

"But then Maddie and Ethan wouldn't be here."

"Oh . . . right." I wonder: Is it better never to have been born if you have to live in a family where Dad beats up Mom?

"On the other hand, there are no strangers, really and truly. Everything and everyone in the universe is related. We're all made of the same star-stuff."

"Even the people who hate me?"

"They don't hate you—some simply don't agree with your viewpoint."

"No, I made a mess of things, and now everyone hates me." And Rawley's at the top of the list, I'm sure of it.

"You've got them thinking, Darya. And the town supervisor's asked you to present your thoughts to the board, so you've really stirred things up." She wraps an arm around me and squeeze-jiggles my shoulder. "You need to learn how to harness your anger and channel it in the right way, that's all. It's okay to be passionate. It's okay to have an opinion. But *filter*. Besides, if everyone agreed with you, you'd be a pretty dull person, in my estimation."

I could burst into tears at any moment. "Yeah, I like that. I like stirring things up." As if

she couldn't tell.

"Me too," she says. "And there's another thing I like."

"What's that?"

She tips her head against mine. "You calling me *Mom*."

I puff out a cloudy breath. The sunbeams have dwindled to occasional flickers of light. A shiver runs down my spine, but it's tamped out by the red flame fueling my heart.

"As long as we're being honest here . . . I always had the feeling that I'd adopted you, but you didn't adopt me back." Mom whooshes out a breath. "There. I've said it."

"Well, let's set the record straight." I take both her hands in my own. "I'm adopting you right *now*."

Mom barks a laugh, then looks up, and scans the sky. The flurries have stopped, at least for now. "Let's do it before it gets too late."

"Do what, Mom?"

"Feed the deer," she says as she trudges toward the house.

While Mom fetches a crate of apples from the garage, I drag my icicle feet upstairs for some dry woolen socks. SpongeBob cackles from the guest bedroom.

I poke my head around the corner. "Hey, you two." Rawley and Maddie are lying belly-down on the bed, eyes glued to the tube, a bowl of goldfish crackers between them. "Where's Libby?"

Rawley leans back on his elbow. His jaw is swollen and purple. Another of Jax's punching-bag victims. "Napping with Ethan. So they're going home?"

"Yep. She's safe now. Jax will be laid up for a long time."

"Sorry I missed the action. I guess I'm not your knight in shining armor."

I stretch out on the bed next to Maddie. She takes a soggy cracker out of her mouth and offers it to me. I jerk my head back, repelled at first, but she grins at me and mushes it against my pursed lips. Oh, what the heck. I open my mouth and take it in. Mothers do it all the time, this intimate exchange of body fluids and germs. Wiping snotty noses with their fingers, eating ice cream off the same spoon, reaching a hand into a diaper to check for poop. I rack it up as practice for when I have my own kids.

Rawley watches as Maddie licks each cracker before feeding it to me. I reach over and run my hand lightly over his jaw. "You okay?"

"Yeah," he says, "thanks, Darya. My head

feels like it's been bashed with a mallet."

It's a shock hearing my name come from his lips. "So why no more Russky now?" I give him a playful shove. "You like me, right?"

"Only because you speak your mind." He looks at me with those dark, soulful eyes, and I get kind of quivery. "That's really attractive. You're your own girl. You don't take crap from anyone—even if I don't agree with half of what you're saying."

The look on his face tells me he's serious. Maybe one day I'll tell him what's really going on inside me. On the surface I project an almost swaggering confidence, but I can't deny that half the time I'm a puddle of tears and indecision on the inside. And what's worse are the mental images of all the times I've cringed when lashing out unfairly at him and Tee-tee.

"How's your mom?" I ask him.

"Good. She's doing real good. The transplant went off with no problem, but she's weak and on antirejection meds. She'll be in the hospital for a while, until she's stable enough to take a plane back home."

Back home to St. Thomas. I'd forgotten that. I finally meet a guy I'm on the verge of really liking, really opening up to, and he's caught in a revolving door, here one minute and gone the

next.

"And you'll be leaving too? Not finishing up the school year here?"

"I'll be flying back with my family. My dad needs help at the dive shop because Mom won't be strong enough to work. My family needs me."

*I* need you. No, that's unfair of me. Of course he needs to help his family. It's not as though I'm the love of his life. We've only known each other a few days, and half that time I've spent despising him.

He gives me a puzzled squint. "What's going through your mind? Is there anything I can do to help?"

"Yes. Be on my side. That would really help."

"You know, I don't think you really need me to be on your side. You've got *you* on your side, and that's worth more than anything a guy like me could give you. I'll be your faithful admirer and foot servant instead. Since I failed my knight exam."

This isn't at all what I'd planned. I don't want someone to wait on me. I want a partner, someone by my side who sees things the way I do and supports me. "*No.* I need you to take my side."

Without a word, Rawley sits up. There, I've

done it again. I've made him angry, and now he's going to leave. He shifts Maddie to his side of the bed and places the cracker bowl in front of her. He swings his legs over Maddie, lightly lifting his body over her small one, and lands with a bounce next to me. He stretches out and aligns himself parallel to me, face to my face. "There. I'm on your side now."

I lean in to kiss him, flu germs be damned.

He pulls back. "Don't. I'm probably still contagious. I have some damn bug."

*Sweet.* This admission makes my day, my week, my year. "A bug? Me too." *Ants in my pants.* I lean in to him again and nuzzle his lips with mine. "Bring it on."

There's something remarkable about being understood, as if you've been stranded on a far-off planet, and some alien finally gets the fact that all you've been asking for is to go home. Rawley is right. I already have someone strong on my side: Me. It's as simple as that, but I was too distracted to let it surface in my brain.

Maddie pops up on her knees. "I have to go poopy. Now."

I tumble over Rawley and scoop Maddie off the bed. "I'll take—"

Rawley lifts her from my arms and glances out the window. "I'll take her. You get out there

with Tee-tee."

"Mom," I tell him. "She's my mom."

He flashes me a grin over his shoulder as he hustles Maddie down the hall, leading her by the hand.

I guess guys *do* know something about kids after all.

*They're coming! The buck swallows his cud and tilts his delicate nose upward. On the brisk north wind, their human scent wafts toward him. The Dar-Ya, and the older one who screeches like an owl. Together.*

*He sniffs again. The wind brings another scent, sweet and fruity. Of the round red globes that grow on trees near the young one's house.*

*The doe steps lightly to his side. She nuzzles the buck's neck. Food, she whistles softly. Dar-Ya offered me food and bestowed her blessing on our young one. She has returned as she promised. She is one of us. She will not hurt us.*

*We must protect her.*

*The buck bows his head and thumps the earth, summoning the others.*

*As the sun dips below the tree line, the herd steps forward to accept their gifts.*

# Don't call me Mom

**I**'ve come to the realization that some of the stories I've relied on to explain who I am have expired. For instance, "Tee-tee is not my real mother" or "Rawley is a deer murderer." Neither of these statements is actually true. What is true is that my birth mother died, my father left me and Nick at an orphanage, and Tee-tee gave us everything a real mother does: food, shelter, and love. A real home and family. Rawley is stuck at his crotchety uncle's house, homesick and worried about his mom. He doesn't murder deer or even dislike them. He was only carrying out his uncle's wishes. These are the facts. I realize now that I'd put my own imagined spin on them, but truth is truth.

But there's one story that hasn't died, that isn't false: The deer need me. I swear I'm not imagining this. It's not like they're my pets and I'm their owner. It's more like *they* own *me*. Or I'm a part of them, a member of their herd in human form. But how could I explain this to anyone? Not Mom or Nick or even Rawley. They'd turn every conversation into a therapy session.

This morning, a few days after the Jax incident, Mom asked me if I'd make dinner for us, just her and me because Nick had been invited to a classmate's birthday dinner. There wasn't much in the fridge, but she said just keep it something healthy and simple, maybe a seven-layer salad with chopped veggies topped with a mix of low-fat sour cream and light ranch dressing. She said she wanted to talk to me about something important. Before I could wheedle it out of her, the school bus honked. Of course all I could imagine was a cancer diagnosis.

So I've made chicken soup with no-yolk dumpling noodles I'd found stashed in the back of the cupboard, past the expiration date, but I can't see any pantry beetle corpses littering the bottom of the cellophane bag, so the noodles meet my quality control standards. Soup is more soothing than salad, and not too heavy. I don't know what she'll be able to eat in the future. I'm

trying hard to stay calm.

Mom doesn't say anything during dinner, and I don't press her. I dread hearing it, the *C* word, but when she finally says it, I plan to act normally and tell her it's something we'll fight—together.

Over coffee she says, "I need to tell you something important, something that affects us both. We need to have a serious talk about this."

I put my hand lightly over hers. "I'm here for you, Mom." I'm in a mild panic. I try to steady myself for the words "breast lump" and "biopsy."

She looks up and smiles. "Well, thank you. But you don't have to look so sad. We both knew the day would eventually come."

First I find out I'm losing Rawley. Now my mom. Two of the three people I care about the most.

"I just didn't expect it would come so soon. I've already lost one mom."

The mug stops halfway to her lips. "I'm not going anywhere. I'm just closing Philoxenia House as of tomorrow."

"Closing—you're not *dying*?"

"Why on earth would you think I was dying?"

The chicken soup churns in my stomach. I'm happy that she's free of the Big *C*, but peeved that she's misled me. "Why wouldn't I? For days all you've been talking about is how you want to eat healthy. And working out at the Y. And getting all New Agey and saying how we're all just specks in a universe that could care less if we live or die."

"Now, sweetie, I didn't say th—"

"And then you want to talk to me privately about something really important, something that affects us both. What *else* was I to think, Tee-tee?"

She gives me one of those tight smiles that doesn't show any teeth. "So it's Tee-tee now, is it? What happened to Mom?"

*Oops.* In the heat of the moment I slipped back into my old ways. "You know what I mean . . . Mom."

She shows me some teeth this time. "It's okay. I'm so accustomed to hearing you call me Tee-tee that Mom seems almost . . . unnatural. I have to look over my shoulder to make sure you're talking to me and not some mother standing behind me."

"So can we please go back to Tee-tee, Mom?"

"Tee-tee it is. But in my heart I'll know that you still think of me as Mom. And maybe when

you're in a moment of sweet disposition—which isn't often, I realize—you might whisper a lovey-dovey *Mom* in my ear. Deal?"

God, I love her. "Deal." But then I remember the real reason why this all came up. "So why are we closing Philoxenia House so soon?"

"After this whole mess with Jax and Libby, I've decided to hang it up. I've been doing this for more than twenty years now, and it's time for someone else to take the reins. There's talk of building a county safe house with all the necessary protective measures installed." She runs her fingertips lightly over my arm. "I'm afraid I've put you and Nikky in danger for much too long."

"Nick," I tell her. "He wants to be called Nick now. Nikky is too babyish."

Tee-tee heaves a sigh. "That's what I mean. You kids are growing up so fast. Pretty soon you'll be graduating and off to college, and Nikky—Nick—will be in middle school and want to hang out with his friends rather than be here with me." Another sigh. "No one will need me anymore."

"We'll always need you. Even if we're not living here. You're our *mother*. And college is eons away."

"I have a surprise for you. When you get

older you'll find out that eons pass in the blink of an eye."

That's impossible. My driver's permit took eons to arrive, the days creeping by at glacier speed.

"You're still going to keep your job at the Helpline, right?" I can't picture Tee-tee sitting around, twiddling her thumbs with nothing to do, or worse, taking up rug-hooking or shuffleboard.

"For a while. But I'm thinking I need to make some changes in my life." She lifts a hand to her head and primps her hair. "Maybe I'll get married."

This is more of a shock than the Big *C* word. "But you're too . . ."

"Say it. *Old*, right? I'll have you know that a nice man at work has asked me out on a date."

I could just about throw up. "Date? A date? A *date*?" I'm sounding like an echo chamber. "Like some old guy—"

"Elderly gentleman . . ."

"—comes to the house and asks my permission to take you for a spin on his walker?"

"Be kind, Darya. Many men in their fifties and sixties are vibrant, intelligent, and fun."

And old. And I'm way too old to have a new

stepfather. I give up my head-on battle and maneuver an attack from the rear. "Maybe all we need is a beach vacation," I say with as much vivacity as I can muster. "Away from all this cold and snow. Winter break's coming up, you know."

"That's a fabulous idea." Tee-tee sits back in her chair and presses a hand over her heart. "Palm trees. Clear blue water. An icy margarita served with one of those little umbrellas by a young muscled beach boy."

That's my Tee-tee. She's back.

She pushes away from the table. "I'll do some online searching right now. Maybe I can get a bargain on airfare if I book right away."

"Go ahead. I'll clean up." I stack the plates and move them to the counter above the dishwasher. "And Tee-tee?"

"Sweetie?"

"I'm so glad you're not dying."

She winks at me. "Me too, sweetie. Me too."

I fill the sink with warm water and squirt in some dish detergent. I immerse the plates in the bubbly water to rinse them off before loading them in the dishwasher, even though the appliance manual says it's not necessary. Tee-tee hates putting food-caked dishes in the dishwasher. She's positive that the dishwasher

whooshes the dirty water around throughout the whole cycle, never rinsing with fresh. She says it's like washing your hair in the tub after you've already taken a bath. I've given up trying to convince her otherwise. Sometimes Tee-tee's like a steamroller, crushing and flattening everything in her way. But I understand now that it's part of what I love about her.

My reflection in the window over the sink is the image of a girl, a real girl without antlers. I know the deer are out there, possibly watching me. Tomorrow I'll feed them with the remaining crate of apples in the garage. They'll be safe on my property, my herd, my family.

"Darya," Tee-tee calls from upstairs.

I wipe my hands on a dishtowel and head for the foyer. Tee-tee's on the landing at the top of the stairs. She holds a printout and taps it with her pencil. "I've printed out a list of beach vacation spots." She scans the sheet through her bifocals. "It looks like we need to fly farther south than Florida to be guaranteed hot weather in December. The Caribbean ranges 80s during the day, 70s at night." She looks up at me. "How does that sound?"

"Super. I'll stash my snow pants and break out the teeny bikini."

"Okay, we need to decide which island deserves our hard-earned tourist money. Do you have a preference? Let's see . . . there's the Caymans, St. Kitts, Jamaica."

Yes. Yes, I do. Rawley stands before me, all sun-kissed shoulders and glorious infuriating grin. "St. Thomas," I call up to her. "St. Thomas will be perfect."

*The herd stands in the field, facing the young human's house. They watch as her face reappears in the kitchen window, a halo brightening her hair from the light above the sink.*

*A doe noses the buck's side. Look how she shines in the light, our Dar-Ya, our Queen. The fruit was so sweet and filling. We will live another day. And she blessed our child. The doe's flanks quiver. He will surely live too.*

*The fawn hobbles up to his mother. Why doesn't she live with us, here among the trees where she belongs?*

*The buck snorts and shakes his crest. She is a young one yet and cannot leave her mother. But soon. Soon she will remember that she is one of us. And she will take her place among us.*

*Whispers arise from the herd. How brave you were to protect her. You saved her, our Dar-Ya.*

*The buck whips his rack back and forth. No. She did not need my protection. She is powerful in herself. I was only protecting her prince. Without him her power is dark, and she cannot shine her message upon the world. With him, she will return to us and light our way.*

*The light above the girl in the window snaps off. A gust of wind whips a swirl of fine snow granules off the roof and sweeps it over the field, blanketing the herd as they kneel and drop to the ground, making their beds in the field. Waiting.*

*Waiting for the day their Dar-Ya will join them.*

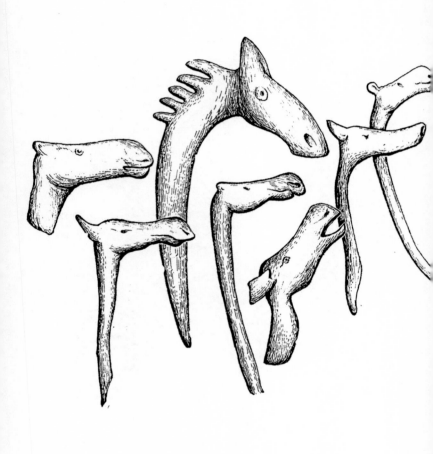

# AUTHOR'S NOTE

*For the Love of Strangers* is a work of fiction inspired by the true story of a relative's trip to Russia, accompanying a friend who traveled there to adopt one child and came back with two siblings. I used my own travels to St. Petersburg, during the White Nights period, and Moscow as a setting backdrop. While some of the facts are true, especially concerning domestic violence victims and deer population culling, most of the plot and all of the characters are imaginary.

The deer antics—busting through glass doors, tangling in Christmas lights, peering into windows, feeding in apple orchards, leaping from highway overpasses, swimming across lakes, attacking humans—are based on actual events experienced by me, told to me by friends, or researched in local news sources.

The domestic violence and shelter thread mirrors the lives of real women facing real problems as discerned from my former work in the human services field.

# Illustrator's Notes

Our cover shows the Paleolithic horned deer goddess with no face to symbolize her universality. In Siberian myth she and her daughter gave birth to the first humans and to the deer herds they lived on. The Mother Deer and her Daughter were named for the Pole stars rather than our Big Dipper. Because she was also worshiped in North America, this deer goddess is shown in Native American dress.

Other prehistoric deer goddesses appear on Siberian deer stones (p. 49) and Bulgarian ceramics (p. 290). To honor her in ritual ceremonies, horses wore horned masks lavishly decorated with gold (chapter headings). Belief in deer goddesses lasted at least a thousand years, as this Scythian jewelry demonstrates (p. 71). Cult deer staffs are found in the graves of women shamans throughout northern Europe (p.

282). Bee goddesses from Anatolia symbolize rebirth after death (p. 134), while the divine tears of a Yugoslavian goddess are the source of life-sustaining water (p.139).

On more modern folk art, horned goddesses with deer are embroidered in red on ritual cloths (title page, text breaks, page headers, and borders), and in spring Ukrainians paint deer on ritual eggs (page numbers and below).

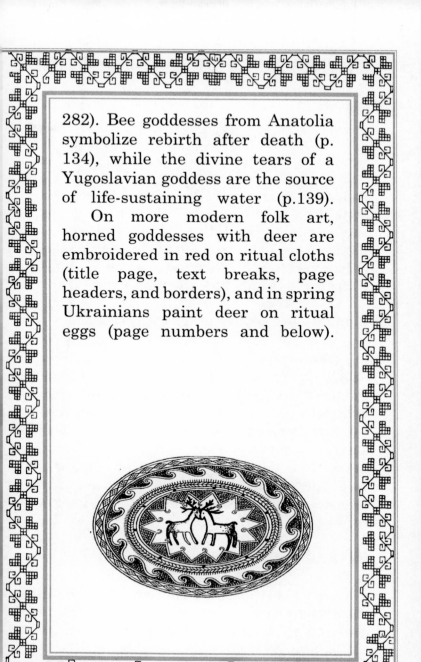

# Discussion Guide – For the Love of Strangers

What is the meaning of the Greek word *philoxenia*?

*Philoxenia* is "the love of strangers" from the Greek *philotis* (love and friendship) and *xenos* (the stranger) and *xenia* (hospitality). The Greek god Zeus is the protector of strangers, and an appeal to *xenios zeus* entitled the stranger to the rites of hospitality. When Odysseus and his comrades are trapped in the Cyclops' cave, Odysseus begs the monster to abide by the rules of *xenios zeus* and offer them hospitality.[1]

How do Darya and Tee-tee practice *philoxenia*?

Darya and Tee-tee (hosts) offer their home as a women's shelter to guests (strangers) in the name of *philoxenia*. According to the ancient rules of hospitality, the host is responsible for the guests under her roof. She must set them safely on their journeys and make sure they reach their destination, because the guest may be a sacred being in disguise, and the host may be entertaining "angels unaware." The guest who receives is not inferior to the host who offers.

What is the mythology behind the characters?

Darya is the reincarnation of Rozhanitza, the ancient Russian deer goddess, the archetypal antlered goddess, giver of birth and death whose

---

1 Lambros Kamperidis, "Philoxenia and Hospitality," *Parabola: The magazine of Myth and Tradition* (Winter 1990): 4–13.

day is the winter solstice. As in every savior story in every culture, Darya must die in order to be reborn. She is the keeper of deer herds, and feeds and protects them. In return, they protect her. Darya stands up for the deer against her community.

Rawley is from the surname Raleigh (RAW-lee), which is from a place name meaning either "red clearing" or "roe deer clearing" or "dweller by the deer meadow" in Old English. Rawley is the deer goddess's prince, her consort, and she is his queen. He accompanies her and lights her way, shining in her darkness, and although she loves him, she does not need him. She is one in herself and powerful without him. He only *enhances* her power. In the story he shows this by supporting Darya and trying to protect her from Jax, even though he fails. Rawley hails from St. Thomas ("Doubting Thomas" was an apostle who doubted Jesus' resurrection when first told of it) in the Virgin (symbolic of goddesses) Islands.

Tee-tee is the embodiment of the Great Mother Goddess. She does not need to bear children, because all the world's beings are her children. In the story Tee-tee loves abused women, children, and even Darya's deer, although she doesn't want to admit it.

How does *philoxenia* play into Darya's protecting the deer?

In sacred literature we have an obligation to show hospitality to all creation—human and nonhuman—and to see ourselves as both strangers and guests on Earth with humility and respect for nature. Darya wants to shelter the deer and is called to protect them as her destiny, as part of a larger plan—the rebirth and return of the savior/host.

Are we all strangers and guests?

Yes, but this doesn't mean we should pull ourselves away and live in a shell. To live as a stranger and a guest means to be dependent on the world, yet have a reverent attitude toward it. Respectful guests don't violate the earth or destroy their home by killing, polluting, or poisoning. Although Darya feels like a stranger, by the story's end she realizes that Tee-tee has always felt like a stranger too. They are both strangers, as are we all, and the realization of this binds them together in a loving relationship.

# Glossary

**Ostav'te menja** *(Ahstahvtyee myeenyah)*—
Leave me alone

**Iditye syouda** *(Eedyeetyee syoodah)*—Come
here

**Nyet** *(Nyeht)*—No

**Dacha** *(Dascha)*—Summer home

**Krasivaya** *(Krahsseevah)*—Beautiful

**Moskovskiy Tsirk**—Moscow Circus

**Spasibo** *(Spahsseebah)*—Thank you

**Stoy. Stoytyee toot.**—Stop. Stop here.

**Tsirk na l'du Ameriki**—Circus on Ice

# ABOUT THE AUTHOR

Jacqueline Horsfall is the author of a dozen joke-and-riddle books, as well as the award-winning nature activity book, *Play Lightly on the Earth*. Jackie and her husband live in the Finger Lakes region of upstate New York, peacefully coexisting with a herd of whitetail deer.

# ABOUT THE ILLUSTRATOR

Mary B. Kelly is a painter, fiber artist, and college art teacher. She is also the author of many articles and books on goddess embroideries. Find out more about her and her creations at marykellystudio.homestead.com/.

Thank you for purchasing this Leap Books publication. For other exciting teen novels, please visit our online bookstore at www.leapbks.com.

For questions or more information contact us at info@leapbks.com

Leap Books
www.leapbks.com

Breinigsville, PA USA
20 October 2010
247671BV00001B/1/P